The
Mistletoe Connection

Chelsea Pennington

First paperback edition December 2020

Cover design by Kyle DeMarco

ISBN: 978-1-0879-1393-3 (paperback)
ISBN: 978-1-0879-1394-0 (ebook)

To Nonny and Poppa.
I love you and I miss you.

Christmas Eve
4:12 pm

Landry's foot bounced as she sat in the hard, plastic seat, connected on either side to identical seats like conjoined twins. Of all the benches scattered across the airport gate, of course Landry would choose the one with the broken plugs. She tapped the screen of her phone again and looked at the battery icon in the top right corner—no lightning bolt signifying it was charging. And she was down to four percent.

Still, she couldn't stop unlocking her phone, lighting up the screen to see if she had any messages. From Mom, she told herself, but Landry knew she was hoping to see a text or even an email from Shelby. It was habit, from a relationship that had almost lasted a year, even as her brain told her heart to get over it. But her heart was stubborn like that.

Landry scanned the seats for an open spot next to an outlet. No luck. Though there weren't many people flying out on Christmas Eve, those who were at the airport had already claimed the chargers. She was debating how far she could go from the gate when an announcement crackled through the speakers.

"All flights out of Denver International Airport have been delayed"—people on all sides of Landry groaned—"due to the current snowstorm. We will keep you informed as we have more information. Thank you for flying out of DIA."

Landry blew out a breath, and a strand of blond hair fluttered off her face. Screw it. She was getting coffee.

She unplugged her phone, gathered everything into her brown canvas backpack, and shoved off the seat. Landry saw other people eying her now-empty spot next to a plug and considered warning them that it was no use, but decided they'd figure it out soon enough.

Despite the airport being emptier than Landry had ever seen, the line at the Starbucks still wrapped around the kiosk. But apparently Landry had nothing better to do with her time, so she stepped up behind a middle-aged man in a suit. Landry understood that some people traveled for business or whatever, but she always relished the opportunity to dress in basically pajamas with almost no chance of seeing anyone she knew. Especially in the Denver airport, it was big enough that she felt comfortable wearing her saggy leggings and a shirt that was two sizes too big with her unwashed hair thrown into a bun. If she had to deal with large amounts of people on their worst behavior while crammed into a metal tube hurtling thousands of feet above the earth, you'd better believe she was going to be comfortable while doing it.

"Landry? Landry Rindall?"

No. No no no no no. Who was here who recognized her?

Plastering a smile onto her face, Landry turned toward the voice.

Directly behind her in line was a white woman in her thirties with shoulder-length brown hair, but she wasn't the speaker. The voice belonged to someone two people behind Landry: a Latina woman with deep brown skin and curly dark hair falling down her back, impeccably dressed in black skinny jeans and a sleek white blouse. She looked familiar, but it couldn't be, surely—

"Landry!" A wide smile lit up the woman's face, and Landry recognized her. It had been ten years, but she would know that smile anywhere.

"Resa?" Landry stepped toward her, but Resa was already lunging forward and scooping her into a hug. Her body was soft and warm and familiar. "It is you!"

Resa laughed. "I got in line and felt like it was you, but then I thought 'what if it's not her and I'm just yelling like some weirdo' but I decided if you *were* here and I didn't say something to you, I'd kick myself later." They had separated and were standing close, still smiling at each other, a few steps away from the kiosk.

"Are you still in line?" The woman who had been in between them, wearing an Arizona Diamondbacks sweatshirt, raised her eyebrows in impatience.

"Oh—you go ahead, I'll hop in behind you with my, uh, friend." It felt weird to call Resa her ex-girlfriend to a random stranger at the airport. Even though that was how they knew each other—girlfriends throughout senior year of high school, before breaking up to avoid a long-distance relationship in college. Landry had always wondered what would have happened if they'd decided to go for it.

She offered the woman a smile, but the woman turned away and stepped forward into what had been Landry's spot.

With raised eyebrows, Landry faced Resa again, and they exchanged a *What's-her-problem* look. A thrill danced through her at the fact that they could still communicate without speaking, edging out any uneasiness she felt.

Resa's smile was dazzling. "Are you flying out tonight? Heading home for Christmas?"

Landry nodded. "You on the flight to Atlanta too?"

"Yep." They shuffled forward as the line moved up. "I was in town for a couple days, but this was the only flight to get home before tomorrow. If it keeps going this way, though, it won't matter anyways." Resa shrugged. "What about you? Why are you flying on Christmas Eve?"

Landry swallowed, images of Shelby's packed bags and Landry's tears and shouted insults from both of them flashing through her mind. She pushed the memory away and simply said, "I had to get a last-minute ticket, and this was the only thing available. But of course Denver would have a blizzard on Christmas Eve." She glanced at Resa. "Why are you in Denver, anyways?"

"Oh, um . . . " Resa stumbled, but then the barista called, "Next!"

Landry turned forward and ordered an Americano. Then she stepped aside and nodded Resa forward. "Also, whatever she's having."

"Oh, Landry, come on," Resa protested, but Landry was shaking her head.

"Nope. My treat. Without this Starbucks line, we might not have met again, so I'm celebrating." Landry grinned at her, and with a small shake of her head and a smile, Resa stepped forward and placed her order.

Landry swiped her card, and they both walked a few feet away to wait for their drinks. The smell of coffee hung in the air, even away from the kiosk, and the moving walkway behind them hummed along, underscoring their conversation with its mechanical whirring.

"Are you looking forward to going back to Atlanta?" Resa asked.

Landry zipped up her wallet and shoved it in her bag. "Mostly, yeah. Like I said, it was a last-minute decision, but it'll be good to see my family."

Resa nodded, but the question was plain in her eyes. Landry prayed she didn't ask it out loud, and her shoulders sagged with relief when Resa just said, "And the bakery?

How's that going?" She grinned. "I have to tell you that I'm obsessed with your Instagram page and all the decorating videos you post."

Landry knew she was blushing, even as her mixed feelings about the bakery she had owned for two years now swirled inside her. "It's going pretty well. Closed it down for today and tomorrow, and then my assistant manager will run it for a couple days until I get back." She tucked some stray hairs behind her ear. "I like it, but it's not like I'm saving lives or anything."

Resa's eyebrows knitted together. "But if you love it, that's what matters, right? And besides"—she winked—"I bet there are plenty of people who would say that your cupcakes are lifesaving. I know I felt that way in high school more than once."

Landry smiled, but inside she squirmed at the compliment. No one actually felt that way, she knew that. Eager to change the subject, Landry planted a hand on her hip. "Can I just say that it is completely unfair that you're flying and you're dressed like that?"

Resa frowned, looking down at her outfit. "Like what? I came to the airport straight from a meeting."

"Exactly!" Landry threw up a hand in exasperation. "You look killer, and I'm dressed like a schlub. If I'd known I was going to run into you, I would've worn something decent."

Resa's laugh was exactly as Landry remembered it, full of warmth with a little hiccupping trill that made it impossible not to join in. "Stop it, you look great." She paused then and held Landry's gaze. "Really great."

Landry knew her cheeks were bright pink, but she was saved from figuring out a response when a barista shouted her name, followed by Resa's. Well, technically the barista said it like *Ray-suh*, when it was actually just the end of Theresa—her full name. Landry made eye contact with Resa, who shook her head with a small, resigned smile. People had been mispronouncing her name since high school.

They grabbed their drinks and then stood in a stilted silence as people rushed by them, the wheels of their suitcases clicking on the tiled floor. Landry wondered where they could be hurrying to—all the flights were delayed, after all.

Resa cleared her throat. "Well, do you want to go sit somewhere? Or do you prefer to drink your coffee while dodging crazed travelers?"

"Oh, yeah, it's my favorite way to pass time in an airport," Landry said lightly. Resa laughed again, and Landry felt a familiar tug in her chest, one that made her want to keep Resa laughing forever.

"Well, I'm not as skilled as you are, so I think we should sit," Resa said, readjusting the shoulder strap of her bag. "Come on, I've got the perfect spot."

Landry raised her eyebrows as she followed Resa. "The perfect spot in an airport?"

Resa's curls bounced as she nodded. "Yep. I do a lot of traveling for conferences and to meet with partner labs and stuff like that, so one way I stay sane is to find a nice nook or chair or something at each airport that feels sort of like . . . my place. Like finding a home no matter where I am." Now she glanced at Landry, uncertainty flickering in her eyes. "That probably sounds super weird or cheesy."

Landry shook her head urgently. "No, not at all. I don't fly that much, but it totally makes sense that you have a routine if you do it a lot."

Resa brightened. "Okay. Thanks. So, yeah, it's just up on the second floor. Since flights are delayed, we'll actually be able to sit and chat. Sometimes I only have ten minutes to sit here, but I'll still do it. It's a chance to breathe. But it's nice when I have a longer gap."

They rode the escalator, Resa one step up from Landry, her body turned so that they could still look at each other as they talked. When they reached the top, Resa strode down a corridor to the right, Landry close at her heels.

After a couple minutes, Resa stopped. "Here it is."

Landry wasn't sure what she was expecting, but it wasn't this. The second floor was bright with the gleaming light reflected off snow in the windows above and shaped like a circle around an opening that looked down to the first floor. Not just the first floor—but an airplane suspended from the rafters, and what appeared to be a garden planted atop the roofs of restaurants and the tram along the lower level. Landry couldn't tell if the plants were real, but it was still a beautiful scene, and the chaos of below disappeared up here, a quiet respite from the bustling travelers. Chairs dotted the second floor, in lines and against the wall.

"Look, I know it's sort of silly, but they're more comfortable than the normal chairs at the gate." Resa plopped down into one of them and pointed at the ground next to her. "And, there's an outlet."

Landry nodded, still looking around. "I think it's great. And I seriously need to charge my phone."

Resa grinned. "All yours."

As Landry yanked her charging cord out of her backpack and settled into the chair next to Resa's, nerves buzzed through her. She hadn't seen Resa since Christmas break of their freshman year of college, and even that had only been across the room at Jen from high school's party. It had been one of those awkward functions that happens on breaks during the first year of college, when everybody is back in their hometown and feels the obligation to try and reconnect, even though hardly anybody wants to be there. They had broken up a month before leaving for college— Landry to University of Colorado Boulder, and Resa to University of Georgia. Even though Landry had spent the semester getting over Resa, when they made eye contact across the room at Jen's party, Landry's body had lurched, as if it would walk to Resa without permission from her brain. But then Resa had given her the same smile she'd given to all the other high school acquaintances at the party.

It seemed like a request for a mutual agreement to let it go. So Landry had.

But now, when she looked up from plugging in her phone, Resa was watching her over the rim of her coffee cup.

"What?" Landry reached a hand up to her high bun. "Is my hair wild? I told you that it's not fair you look good and I—"

"Stop," Resa said with a laugh. "I . . . It's nice. Being here with you. I've kept up with you on Instagram and stuff, but I never thought I'd get to just . . . be with you. Talking, like this. I've missed it."

Landry's cheeks heated again. "Oh. Well, me too." Then her grin slipped into something more mischievous. "Although, it's not like we did all *that* much talking when we were in high school. I seem to remember us being busy with *other* things."

Resa's jaw dropped, but her eyes danced, and Landry's chest swelled at the fact that she could render Resa speechless like that. She couldn't help it—she laughed. "Your face! You look so scandalized."

Resa swatted at her shoulder. "Shut up. I don't remember you being so . . . "

"Witty?"

"Annoying," she settled on, but the smirk on her face told a different story. Landry wasn't sure what to do with the fluttering feeling that the look produced in her stomach.

Resa sipped her coffee. "So . . . are you seeing anyone? I've seen pictures of you with that one girl for a while."

Landry sucked in a breath, the flutters in her stomach doused. "Oh, yeah, um, Shelby. We're not . . . I mean, we broke up. So, no, I'm not seeing anyone." She focused on her phone, avoiding Resa's piercing gaze.

Resa was quiet for a moment, then said, "Well, it's her loss."

Landry rolled her lips inward to bite them. She wasn't sure about that. And she definitely knew Shelby didn't feel that way.

But she didn't want to think about that anymore. So Landry cleared her throat and asked, "What about you? Seeing anyone?" She drank from her coffee cup, savoring the bright bitterness on her tongue, trying to look casual, like Resa's answer didn't really matter to her.

Resa shook her head, crossing one leg so that her right foot rested on her left knee as she spoke. "Nope." She lifted her shoulder in a half-hearted shrug. "My job keeps me super busy, and relationships just haven't worked out with my weird schedule." She tucked a curl behind her ear. "Most people want to spend their weekend going to the farmer's market or something, not in a lab studying moss."

Landry laughed. "I have to say, I'd choose the farmer's market between the two. But you've always been the nerdy one." Resa chuckled. Landry smiled at her, but it felt tight. For a moment, she had forgotten that Resa was kind of a big deal in the environmental biology world, a distinguished professor at Mercer University, and traveling all over to do research and speaking engagements. She swallowed, suddenly feeling like a sweater that shrunk several sizes in the wash.

"Landry?"

Her head snapped up at Resa's voice.

"You okay?" Concern filtered into Resa's face, and Landry once again forced a smile.

"Yep! Sorry, just tired. I'm fine though." Landry pushed aside thoughts of Resa's job, and Shelby, and her anxieties about her own future, hoping all those small doubts would go quiet if she could only ignore them long enough.

4:23 pm

Adrian stared out the large window that ran along the side of the gate, watching the snow spin in the wind. He'd sometimes hated snow while he'd lived in Colorado, but now he wondered when he would see it again.

"Adrian, can you help me with this? My iPad won't connect." His mom broke into his thoughts as she turned from the seat next to him and held out her tablet to him, helpless.

He held back a sigh as he took it from her. "Look, it's this little icon in the corner. See?"

"*Adrian.*" Mariel was seventeen and he was fifteen, but sometimes she acted like more of a mom than their actual mom. At this exact moment she was glaring at him from a few seats over. "Don't be sassy to her. Just do it, okay?"

Adrian gritted his teeth. "I'm trying to show her so she can do it herself next time."

"Stop talking about me like I'm not here," his mom interrupted. "I'm sitting in between you."

13

"Sorry," they both murmured.

Mariel turned back to their younger sister, Sofia. She was only six, and though Mom and Dad wouldn't say it, Adrian and Mariel knew she had been a surprise baby. Adrian had been unsure about getting a baby sister when he was already nine, but now he couldn't imagine life without her.

"See, what does this say?" Mariel pointed at a word in the picture book she held in front of Sofia.

"T-t . . . " Adrian couldn't help but smile as Sofia's mouth work up and down, trying to pronounce the word.

His phone buzzed, drawing his attention. It was an Instagram notification—someone had commented *we'll miss you!* on the photo he'd taken of the snow on their ride in, with a short caption about leaving behind Colorado. Instead of the usual small thrill at the alert, Adrian's stomach sank. For a second, he'd almost been able to pretend they were just traveling for the holidays, not moving out of the country. He'd almost been able to leave behind the sinking feeling of walking into a dark room without knowing where any of the furniture sat or where the light switch was.

Adrian ran a hand through his dark hair and stood up. "I'm gonna go for a walk."

Mom eyed him. "Where are you going?"

He shrugged, shoving his hands into the pockets of his jeans. "Nowhere. Maybe I'll grab a snack."

"Hey, get me a bag of Chex Mix," Mariel said without looking up from the book with Sofia.

"Lazy," Adrian called to her.

"Rude."

"Hey!" Mom interrupted. "Get your sister her snack. Don't go too far. We don't know when our flight will take off."

Adrian glanced back out at the window, where it was hard to tell where the white sky ended and the snow-covered earth began. He nodded, but thought to himself that it didn't look like their flight was going to be leaving anytime soon.

"'Kay. I'll be back in a little bit." He grabbed his phone and hurried away from the chairs before anyone could stop him.

Adrian pulled out his earbuds and stuck them in his ears as he started walking through the terminal. His mouth salivated when he passed by a shop selling warm pretzels, glistening with butter in the florescent lights. But he didn't feel like he could eat anything right now, with the knot that his stomach had tied itself into. Ever since he learned they were moving, it seemed like his stomach hadn't been able to *un*knot. Now that they were actually here, in the airport . . . Adrian wasn't sure if his stomach would ever be the same.

He stared at the gray carpet under his feet, the swirling pattern on it blurring as he hurried through the terminal, dodging the few other travelers. It wasn't just that they were leaving—though that seriously sucked. But the people he went to school with, people he might have called friends . . . did any of them actually care if he left? He had never really clicked with anybody at his school. Sure, he had people to sit with at lunch, and a few guys he played video games with online on the weekend sometimes. But when he found out he was leaving, when he told everyone at lunch . . . All their responses had felt empty. Like, sure, they might miss him at first, but no one would remember him by March. He hadn't left a mark on anyone, and his spot in the group would feel less like the gap left by a missing tooth, and more like a thumbprint in Play-Doh: easily filled in and molded over.

Which left him with one looming question: If he hadn't been able to make real friends at a school where he knew most of the people since middle school, how was he supposed to fit in as the new kid at a school in Spain?

The question had plagued his thoughts for months now, lurking in the corners of his mind until it jumped out at the most inopportune moments. Now it wouldn't stop spinning in his head, like a website trying to load with bad internet connection that got stuck in an endless loop. Adrian turned up the volume on his music, trying to drown everything out, including his own thoughts. It didn't help.

Adrian, eyes trained on the ground in front of him and music blaring, kept walking faster and faster, as if he could outrun his mind. He might have actually broken into a full run, but before he could, he came around the corner of a kiosk and slammed into someone.

"Whoa, there!" The voice belonged to an older white man, who had thrown out a hand to catch himself on the wall of the kiosk.

Adrian's face flushed with shame, and he went rigid, waiting for the man to start yelling as he yanked out his earbuds. "Shoot—I'm sorry, I wasn't paying attention—"

"It's all right." The man smiled kindly at him, and Adrian relaxed. No one appeared from the other side of the kiosk to see what happened, so he thought it must be closed, or they really didn't care. "Are you okay?"

Adrian stuffed his earbuds into his pockets. "Yeah. I'm all good."

The man, who wore a blue sweater vest, nodded. "No harm done, then. Just be careful next time, all right?"

"Yeah. Thanks." He smiled tightly, lips pressed into a thin line.

The man smiled at him—a real smile, not like Adrian's embarrassed one, he noted—and walked off, leaving Adrian standing there, unsure what to do now. At least that had distracted him.

Up ahead, he spotted a store that seemed to sell a little bit of everything, including snacks. He remembered Mariel had told him to get Chex Mix, so he wandered toward the store, hoping to find another distraction before his mind started to spin out once again.

4:30 pm

In the Snax 'N' More at the airport, there were no windows, or even exterior walls. But Kat had figured out that if she stood behind the counter with the cash register one step to her left, and the display of tissue packs two steps to her right, she could peek up on her tiptoes above the tall rack of magazines and see a sliver roughly two square inches of the window by the nearest gate. This was how she knew it was snowing, bad.

That, and her phone kept dinging with texts and weather alerts warning her of the impending blizzard.

She sighed and leaned against the counter. A steady trickle of people had been coming through all afternoon, and she expected it would only increase before her shift ended at six, but for now there was a lull. Christmas music played on a low volume through the speakers, though she did her best to tune it out since it was the same dozen songs on repeat. Kat tapped her fingernails, painted a deep purple that stood out against her pale skin, on the counter before unlocking her phone and checking her email. Still nothing.

She blew out a breath and opened Instagram. Everyone's photos were celebrating the snow, and several had videos with some version of "White Christmas" playing. Kat rolled her eyes. Easy to love the snow when it's not going to get you stuck at work.

"Excuse me, ma'am, can you get off your phone and do your job?"

Kat's head snapped up, even though she recognized the voice. "You suck," she said, throwing a pack of travel-sized tissues at the speaker: Trevor, who worked across the walkway at The Slice and also happened to be her best friend since seventh grade.

Trevor cackled as he hopped up to sit on the counter. "You were pissed for a second there."

"Whatever, dude." Kat rolled her eyes. "Did they let you off early?"

"I wish." Trevor grabbed a magazine someone had left on the counter and flipped through it idly. "Nah, it's super slow, so I figured I'd come say hi."

"More like come use my discount to buy some crap." Kat folded her arms and raised an eyebrow.

He looked up from the magazine with wide eyes, feigning innocence. "What? I would never."

"Don't you lie to me."

Trevor slapped the magazine closed. "Okay, you got me. Can I get some Sour Patch Kids?"

"Fine."

He jumped off the counter to walk to the candy section.

"Do you really think they'll make us stay here even with the snow?" Kat asked.

Trevor skimmed the shelves looking for the package, then grabbed it and brought it to the counter. "You kidding me? With all these flights delayed and probably canceled and people who will need food? We're gonna be here forever."

Kat groaned as she scanned the barcode and then typed in her employee number to get the ten percent discount. "My shift ends at six." She slid the bag of candy across the counter to him.

"Yeah, I'm off at seven, but by then I don't know if the roads are gonna be good enough even for buses. This is supposed to get real bad. Don't hold your breath for them letting us off early to get home." Trevor, leaning forward against the counter, tore open the packaging and popped a candy in his mouth.

Kat let out a sigh. She had agreed to work Christmas Eve to get the holiday pay, but she would have tried to get out of it if she knew it would mean getting snowed in like this. She watched Trevor eat some more of the candy.

"What do you think the singular form of Sour Patch Kids is?" Kat mused as she held her hand out toward him.

Trevor rummaged through the bag until he found a couple of yellow ones and plopped them into her waiting palm. "Wouldn't it be 'Sour Patch Kid'? No plural kids?"

"I guess." Kat chewed. "But is it still capitalized like the brand name? Or is it different?"

Trevor frowned. "I'm . . . not sure."

Kat had another thought, but before she could voice it, her phone pinged again. Her eyes flickered down to the screen, hoping for an email, but it was a text.

"Is it what's-her-face?" Trevor's voice made her look up.

"What?" She frowned, fingers poised over her screen.

"The text. Is it from that girl you've been seeing?" His eyes stayed focused on the bag of Sour Patch Kids.

Kat shook her head. "I didn't tell you? We—well, not broke up, because we weren't ever really dating, but we haven't hung out in a while. She kept saying her job was super busy, but it's whatever." She gave a one-shoulder shrug and looked back at her phone.

Trevor ate another piece of candy, placing it thoughtfully in his mouth before chewing. "So who're you texting? Another girl? Some guy?" Trevor had been the first person she came out to as bisexual, but sometimes he acted like her mom with all the questions.

Kat laughed. "Will you chill? It's my mom, asking if I'm gonna try to catch the bus or if I want a ride from her."

"Doesn't she live, like, forty minutes away from your apartment?"

"Yeah, but you know. Moms." She locked her phone. "I don't want her driving in this, though. I'll take the bus, or I guess spend the night here." Kat stuck her tongue out at the idea.

Trevor shrugged as he looked down, fiddling with the plastic packaging. "I dunno, that could be kind of fun. At least we'd both be here, to hang out together."

"Yeah, I mean I'm glad it's you working and not Weird Lance." They laughed, thinking of another employee at The Slice who always gave Kat bad vibes.

Just then, a kid meandered into the store through the entrance directly across from the counter. He had tan skin and dark hair that curled just above the tips of his ears.

"Okay, get out of here," Kat shooed Trevor away. "Some of us actually have to work."

He made an overly surprised face. "Is that what you do here all day? Shoot, I thought you just gave out free candy."

"I'm gonna smack you," she threatened as he grinned at her.

"I'm leaving, I'm leaving!" Trevor held up his hands in a show of surrender, one still holding the bag of candy. "See you later."

"Later," she called.

The kid had grabbed a bag of Chex Mix from the snack section, but instead of coming up to the counter, he browsed the shelves of books. It was the one part of the store that she actually paid close attention to how well it looked, making sure all the covers faced the right way. She liked to imagine her name among them someday, people coming across her book as they browsed during a layover.

Deciding that the kid wasn't going to check out anytime soon, Kat took her phone back out and opened up the Google Docs app. She clicked over to the short story she'd been working on about a girl who befriended dragons. Like Khaleesi from *Game of Thrones*, but the dragons were more like big puppies that could breathe fire. She would never show it to anyone—other than Trevor, of course—but it was a nice way to escape the monotony of working retail.

She had gone to college and gotten an English degree, and so for a long time she'd tried to write Literary-with-a-capital-L fiction. But she nearly bored herself to tears writing it, so she decided to write something like the books she actually enjoyed reading and discovered it was a great way to pass the time. Kat was grateful to Trevor for getting her this job—he'd worked here since graduating high school, then left to The Slice since it paid more, but not before recommending her to the manager here after she graduated college. It was better than nothing and the pay wasn't terrible, but it could be the most boring place. Which gave her a lot of time to write.

Writing also helped with her anxiety, at least sometimes. So much of the world was out of her control, and sometimes it seemed like even her brain was out of her control, too. She couldn't keep up with the thoughts that bombarded her mind, worries about her personal life and the people she loved and huge, global issues she couldn't do anything about. But with writing, she could create her own world and escape into a place where she had complete control. It kept her mind straight and her breathing steady. Sometimes it was the only thing that could do that.

When Kat glanced up from her phone again, another customer had entered. This time it was an older white man wearing a blue sweater vest who reminded Kat a little bit of her grandpa. He browsed for a few minutes before picking out a Milky Way candy bar and a box of Milk Duds and brought them to the counter.

"Got a chocolate craving?" Kat joked as she scanned the items. In her one-year performance review last week, her boss, a Black woman named Helena, insisted she be more "personable" to the customers, so Kat was trying to figure out small talk.

The man smiled at her, as if he somehow knew exactly what she was doing. "I do have a sweet tooth, but the Milk Duds are for my daughter. I'm flying to spend Christmas with her and her family, and thought I might bring her something. Besides all the Christmas presents, I guess."

Kat nodded, her smile more genuine as she took the ten-dollar bill he handed to her. "That's sweet. Where does she live?"

"Atlanta." He glanced toward where the window would be, if you could see it from his angle. "Although, with all this snow, I'm not sure I'll actually make it out there."

He tapped the box of Milk Duds on the counter. "Might have to eat these myself."

Kat laughed. "What a sacrifice."

He winked at her. "One that I'm willing to make if needed." He nodded at her as he turned to go. "Merry Christmas."

"Merry Christmas," she called, wishing all customers could be as easygoing as he was.

Kat looked around the store and saw the kid was still there. The bag of Chex Mix lay, seemingly forgotten, on the shelf in front of a James Patterson book, while he leaned against the wall, absorbed in a graphic novel. He didn't seem like the type to steal anything, but she kept an eye on him anyways. There was only one other person in the store, a white girl around the boy's age, who had just walked in and was browsing the magazine section.

Sliding one step to the right, Kat stood on her tiptoes to get a peek out the window. Still snowing hard. With a sigh, she opened up her phone and checked her email. Nothing new. She switched to her story and kept writing.

4:35 pm

June nearly didn't notice the boy at first. She had wandered into the store mostly out of boredom during a short walk to stretch her legs. It was weird being at the airport without her parents, and the excitement of flying by herself for the first time had continued to wear off the longer her flight was delayed. Now she wandered along a row of magazines, not really taking in the glossy covers and photos of celebrities.

When June got to the end of the row, instead of looking at George Clooney's face, she startled at the real-life human in front of her. A boy around her age with curly dark hair who happened to be kinda cute.

He didn't even look up from what he was reading, despite June standing less than three feet away. She frowned as she craned her neck to see exactly what he was reading— and gasped.

That got his attention. He looked as surprised to see her standing there, way too close to him, as she had felt when she first saw him.

"Um, hi?" His voice was quiet but confused, his hands still holding onto the open graphic novel.

"Hi!" June said. He took a half-step back, and June knew she was talking too loudly, but that's what happened when she got nervous. "Sorry, um, this is weird, but are you a Golden Hollow fan?" She nodded to the graphic novel he had been so absorbed in.

There was a pause, and a wave of embarrassment washed over June. Maybe he had just picked it up, maybe he was silently laughing at how weird it was, and now he was trying to decide how to tell her she was a dork for liking a graphic novel; no, he'd probably call it a *comic book* with a voice that dripped disdain—

"Yeah, they're, like, the only thing I read," he said with a laugh. "Sorry, it took me a second. I was like, *how did she know that* and then I realized I'd been reading one. Duh." His laugh sounded a little nervous, but it was still a nice laugh. June smiled as she tucked a piece of her auburn hair behind her ear.

"No, I've totally done stuff like that before. Like someone asks if I like a band and I think they're a mind reader before I remember I'm wearing a shirt from their concert or something." She smiled at him, and he returned it. "I'm June."

"Adrian." He lifted up the book. "So, you like Golden Hollow too?"

27

She nodded. "I'm obsessed. But I've never actually met anyone else who reads them. There's a group on Tumblr that I freak out over them with, but that's it."

"Well, it's good to meet you, then. This is the newest one—have you read it yet?" Adrian tilted the cover to face her more. "*The Dubious Dilettante.*"

June shook her head. "Not yet. I pre-ordered it, but it arrived at my mom's house in Georgia, and I've been at my dad's place here, so . . . "

"Gotcha. Yeah, I put a hold on it at our library, and there's, like, fifteen people in front of me." He stuck a hand in the pocket of his jeans. "So I thought I'd start reading it here when I saw it, but then I guess I got a little carried away." His cheeks turned a light shade of pink, and the sheepish look on his face was so cute that June's stomach did a little flip-flop.

Trying not to think about that, she nodded, her wavy hair nearly bouncing from her enthusiasm. "I mean after the cliff-hanger from the issue before—"

Adrian's eyes widened. "Exactly! I almost threw the book across the room when I turned the page and realized there wasn't anything else after it."

June laughed. She had nearly done the same thing herself. "On Tumblr we've all been trying to guess what comes next, but I'm sure none of us are right."

"Any leading theories you have?" He raised his eyebrows. "I can tell you how close you are."

June was about to launch into a description of one she had found convincing, but her phone buzzed at that moment, drawing her thoughts away. June glanced at it and let out an involuntary groan.

"Everything okay?" Adrian's head tilted to the side, concern written all over his face.

"Yeah," June muttered, staring at the text.

baby, you can't ignore me forever. can't we talk??

She swallowed. How many times did she have to tell him there was nothing to talk about?

"Are you sure?"

Her head snapped up as she looked at Adrian. Even with—and maybe especially because of—the concern creasing his forehead as he studied her, he was pretty cute. An idea sparked in her mind, and she grinned. "Hey—I know we just met, but do you want to help me with something?"

The concern transformed into something that June thought could either be curiosity or wariness. "What kind of something?"

June held up her phone. "This text is from my ex-boyfriend. I dumped him last week because . . . well, because. But he won't leave me alone." She raised an eyebrow. "*But* if he thought I'd met someone new and moved on . . . "

Adrian was frowning now. "You . . . want me to pretend to be your boyfriend?"

June nodded. "Something like that. We hang out together, and I'll take some pictures and post them on

29

Instagram. He'll see them and back off." She smiled at him hopefully, clasping her hands together in a pleading gesture. "What do you think? We're stuck here anyways, right? I'm bored out of my mind, and this sounds like way more fun than sitting and waiting for them to decide to let the flight take off."

Adrian shifted his weight, but then nodded. "Yeah. Okay. Sure."

"Great!" June beamed. "Where should we go first?" Then she nodded at the book he was still holding. "Oh—are you going to buy it? Looks like it's the only copy left."

"Oh, um." He shook his head, holding it out to her. "No, you go for it."

June held up her hands in a *not me* gesture. "No, seriously, you found it first. All yours. Like I said, I've got a copy waiting for me, if I ever get out of this airport."

Adrian chewed on his lip. "How about I buy it, but then we can, um, sit and read it together?" He didn't meet her eyes when he said it, instead studying the cover.

She grinned. "Brilliant." Now Adrian looked up, a smile tugging at his lips. "Kaden—that's my ex's name—never understood why I liked Golden Hollow, so if I post a picture of us reading together, it'll drive him nuts. I'll buy us reading snacks!" June grabbed a pack of Skittles and a package of peanut butter crackers. "Is that Chex Mix yours?" She nodded to a bag sitting on the shelf by the empty spot where *The Dubious Dilettante* had been.

"Nope, I don't need it." Adrian put the bag back on the snacks shelf on their way up to the counter.

A twentysomething white woman with hair that was deep black with a sheen of blue looked up from her phone as they approached. "Find everything?" she drawled as if she'd said it more times than she could count that day.

"Absolutely," June said as she set the snacks on the plastic-topped counter. She paid for them with the card her mom had given her with the instructions that it was for emergencies only. June figured being snowed in at an airport was close enough. She waited as Adrian bought the graphic novel.

"Where do you want to go?" Adrian asked as they emerged from the store. "Do you need to tell your parents or anything?"

June shook her head as she walked toward a map of the terminal, Adrian following her. "Nope. I'm traveling by myself. Unaccompanied minor. What about you?" She searched the map, though it only showed restaurants and stores, not anything helpful for a place to sit and hang out.

Adrian's eyebrows rose. "That's cool. Yeah, I'm with my family. But they'll be fine." He glanced at the map, and when he frowned, June assumed he had reached the same conclusion she had. "This isn't helpful. Come on." He turned toward their right. "Let's go this way and see what we can find."

He set off, and June trotted behind him, her boredom most definitely cured.

4:47 pm

Charles let out a sigh as he eased himself back down onto the chair after throwing away the wrapper for his Milky Way bar. His daughter, Shonda, would lecture him if she knew he'd eaten the chocolate, but she was in Atlanta, and what she didn't know wouldn't hurt her.

The sun was already starting to set outside, and the final remnants of the weak winter light filtered in through the windows, casting everything in a pale white. He was seated at the end of the terminal, with several gates facing each other and rows of chairs crossing the space in between. From what he could tell, people from several different flights were all mixed together here. On the opposite end of the row where he sat was a couple who looked to be in their thirties and occasionally glanced at the gate for the Seattle flight. The white woman wore a Diamondbacks sweatshirt and her eyes regularly flickered over to look at the man, who had warm bronze skin and might have been Asian. He was on his phone and seemed to be studiously ignoring her.

Across the aisle in the chairs facing him was a family, the two parents talking with each other, and the two daughters each absorbed in their own activity. The oldest had been reading to the youngest earlier, but now the oldest was on her phone, and the younger girl flipped through the book on her own, too fast to actually be reading. She closed the book abruptly and caught Charles looking at her. She smiled at him in the unabashed way that only children can. He smiled back, reminded of his own grandkids.

"Hi," she called across the aisle. Her long dark brown hair was pulled back into a ponytail. "What's your name?"

"Sofia, shh. Leave him alone," the older sister said. She glanced at Charles. "Sorry. Bit of a social butterfly."

Charles laughed. Very similar to his oldest granddaughter, then. "No worries." He looked at the youngest, Sofia. "My name is Charles. And you're Sofia?" She nodded. "That's a very pretty name. How old are you?"

"Thank you. I'm six years old, and I'm learning to read. Kylie can read a whole Boxcar Children book, but I'm still reading Nate the Great. It's funny. I like it." She rattled off all this information in one breath. Charles's smile grew.

"That's still very impressive. Is Kylie your sister?" Charles guessed.

"No, that's Mariel. Kylie is my friend in class. But we're moving, so I won't see her again for a long time." Sofia's face fell a little at this. "I don't want to move. I like our home."

Charles nodded, filled with understanding. "That's okay to feel that way. Moving can be scary. Can I tell you something?" Sofia nodded energetically, and he leaned forward a little. "My daughter wants me to move, too, but I want to stay where I live now in my house. So I guess I'm a little scared of moving too."

Sofia frowned as she considered this. "But you're grown up. You don't have to move, right?"

Charles chuckled. "Sometimes even grown-ups have to do things they don't want to do." He settled into his chair. His back could only take so much.

Before Sofia responded, her parents looked up and noticed her and Charles speaking.

"Shh." The woman turned to face her daughter. "Stop bothering the man."

"It's really okay," Charles said, now smiling at the woman. "She reminds me of my granddaughter, Monica."

The woman smiled. "She's chatty, too?" She was wearing a red sweater and dark blue jeans.

Charles nodded. "Oh, yes. The girl could talk to a wall and get it to respond. Never met a stranger, that one."

"Sounds like they would be friends," the man said with a smile. "I'm Jon. This is my wife, Ellen." His daughters clearly took after him, with the same tan skin, dark hair, and straight nose.

"Charles." He readjusted his position, crossing his right leg over his left. "Are you traveling for Christmas?"

"Something like that," Ellen said. "Heading to see family in Boston first, then on to Spain." Her gaze shifted toward her oldest daughter, still on her phone a few chairs away. For a moment, something like uncertainty and worry flashed across her face, but then she looked back at Charles and it was gone, replaced with the same warm smile.

Charles wondered what that meant, but simply asked, "Ah. Is it nice there this time of year?" He realized he didn't really know much about the country.

The man, Jon, nodded. "It's chilly for Spain, but still in the fifties. So definitely warmer than here."

Ellen laughed, tucking her light brown hair behind one ear. "We've lived in Colorado for years, and the winters never get any better."

"Oh, yes, that's true." Charles shook his head. "My wife and I moved to Denver forty years ago from Texas, and we were shocked when we woke up one day in October to six inches of snow!" They all laughed.

"Where's your wife?" Jon said, still smiling.

Charles swallowed down the lump in his throat. He knew it was a logical question to ask, but he always dreaded the answer. "Passed away earlier this year. Cancer."

Ellen made a small, sympathetic noise, the kind he'd grown used to hearing over the past several months. "I'm so sorry. This is your first Christmas without her, then?"

Charles nodded. "Christmas was her favorite time of year . . . " He wanted to say more, but his throat was tight.

Ellen nodded. "Christmas is hard. So many happy people, but it only makes your sadness feel worse." She smiled at him, but it wasn't laced with pity like he'd come to expect. Though he couldn't speak yet, he smiled back and felt like she understood.

4:52 pm

Keely twisted and untwisted the strings of her Diamondbacks sweatshirt around her finger. The red rope coiled around, then released back into a straight line. She glanced at Wes again, but his eyes stayed focused on his phone. Keely sighed, but her husband didn't look up.

She stared out the window at the snow coming down in what looked more like sheets of white than individual snowflakes. Why did they have to have a layover in Denver? Why not some place warm? When they'd left Phoenix early this morning, it had been in the seventies.

Another glance at Wes. Still on his phone. She was pretty sure they'd spoken fewer than five sentences to each other since getting through security. It made her want to grab the phone from his hands, to do the chicken dance, something to make him look up.

But she didn't. Of course. Keely sat there and played with her sweatshirt, her book in her lap. She kept trying to read, but every time she picked the book up, her eyes glazed over and the words blurred together until she realized she'd been reading the same sentence for the past five minutes.

She yawned. They had both been up late last night, neither willing to give in to the other by going to bed, and she'd been counting on sleeping on the plane. Now she was stuck in this airport and would rather go direct traffic on the runway in a blizzard than lay her head on Wes's shoulder to nap.

Keely tried to take a drink of her iced latte from Starbucks but discovered that it was nearly empty. Her straw made an ugly sucking noise as she scraped the dregs of the whipped cream from the bottom.

Now Wes looked up. "Could you not do that?"

Keely shrugged, still trying to reposition her straw to where a few puffs of whipped cream remained. "I'm trying to get the last of it. It's almost gone."

"Straws don't make that noise if there's anything left," Wes snapped. His fingers clenched the sides of his phone.

"Fine." Keely pushed herself out of the seat and walked to the trash can, passing by the few other people in the chairs for surrounding gates. An elderly man. A family that included a young girl who was singing to herself as she played some game on an iPad. The plastic rattled as she tossed the cup in the recycling bin.

When she returned to her seat, Wes was on his phone again. Keely slumped into her chair, letting out a loud sigh.

"What," Wes's voice was flat, emotionless.

Keely swallowed. She'd never heard him like this. "Nothing. I'm just tired of waiting. I want this plane to either leave or get canceled so we can find a hotel or something." She tapped her fingers on the plastic armrest, chin resting in her other hand.

"It all depends on the weather. They'll tell us whenever they know something."

Keely rolled her eyes even though Wes wasn't looking. "Oh really? Is that what happens?"

Wes glanced at her. "You're the one complaining about something out of our control."

"Yeah, that's how complaining *works*," she shot back, even as she knew she was being childish.

Wes blew out a breath. Keely tensed, wondering if he would finally break, but he simply said, "All right," and went back to his phone.

Keely wanted to argue, wanted to keep prodding him until he snapped and they yelled at each other like last night, but she was very aware of the young girl from the family a few chairs down watching them with interest now. So she leaned back in her chair and chewed on her lip, wishing to be anywhere else but here.

5:11 pm

Adrian wiped his palms on his jeans once again. Ever since he started talking to June in that store, his hands had been clammy. His stomach felt like a Boy Scout was practicing knots on his intestines. He and June were sitting on the ground of an empty gate, their backs up against the thick glass that overlooked swirling snow obscuring the tarmac. The glossy pages of the graphic novel flashed in the dim gray light coming in through the window as he turned them. June was sitting so close he could smell her shampoo—something bright and tropical, maybe coconut?— -and he was very aware that if he scooted an inch to the right, their arms would touch. He swallowed.

Right after they'd sat down, June had arranged them for a photo—her head on his shoulder, the Golden Hollow book clutched against her chest, Adrian's face not quite in the frame.

"It can't seem like I'm bragging about hanging out with a guy, or he'll know I'm making it up," June explained as she edited the photo for Instagram. "I'm gonna write something about finding the new Golden Hollow novel,

40

and it'll just be obvious that I'm also very cozy with the person I'm reading it with."

Adrian was amazed by how girls' minds worked, and also a little pissed that she had to go through so much trouble to get her ex to leave her alone. He was also trying to ignore how his heart seemed to stumble when she leaned her head against him like they'd known each other forever.

Since then, they had been sitting and reading together for nearly half an hour, the quiet only broken by sporadic comments about the novel and the sound of crunching on the snacks, which they'd finished awhile ago. Now June leaned back and let out a sigh. "Okay, I feel like we should savor this. Who knows how long we'll be stuck here?"

Adrian laughed—it was still higher pitched than his regular laugh, but his nerves didn't seem to allow him to laugh normally—and closed the graphic novel with a *thwapping* sound. "So what do you want to do?"

"Figured we could talk." She bounced her foot up and down. Adrian had noticed she did that, constantly tapping her foot to a rhythm, as if she were dancing to music no one else could hear.

June swiveled her head to face him. "You said you're flying with your family? Where are you going?"

The question was a natural one to ask, but it still caught Adrian off guard. "Um, Boston."

"Cool. Do you have family there? Or is that where you live and you were just visiting here?"

Adrian winced at these questions. They were expected, but he sort of hated talking about leaving Colorado. And he didn't know how she'd react. So he dodged.

"I'm boring. What about you? You said your mom is in Atlanta?" He forced his voice to be light and airy.

June eyed him, as if she knew what he was doing, but allowed it. "Yeah. My parents are getting a divorce. I mean, they've been separated for almost a year, but now they're actually about to finalize it." She twisted a loose thread from the hem of her T-shirt around her finger. "My dad moved to Denver a couple months ago when his job transferred him, and my mom stayed in Atlanta. So now instead of driving across town, I get to fly halfway across the country for a visit." She laughed, but it sounded hollow.

"That sucks, I'm sorry." Adrian chewed on the inside of his cheek, not sure what else to say. "So you're visiting your mom for Christmas?"

"Yeah. It's all kinds of weird, because normally divorced kids do, you know, Thanksgiving with one parent and then Christmas with the other, and swap. But I had this big tournament over Thanksgiving break—I do speech and debate—so I didn't really spend it with either of them, so there was this big fight over who 'got' me for Christmas, like I'm some toy. I mean, they never fought in front of me on purpose, but I could hear phone calls and stuff." June tucked her hair behind one ear and looked down. "Finally I told them that I'd stay with Dad for the start of winter break up to Christmas Eve, then fly to Mom for Christmas Day and the last half of break." She snorted. "It's a bad idea, and I knew it was bad when I suggested it. I think I was sort of hoping it'd be like that story about the king—Solomon, with the moms fighting over the baby, you know?"

"Um, maybe?" Adrian said, shifting so he could face her better.

"So there's this super wise king, and two women come to him claiming that the same baby is theirs. He says to chop the baby in half and each woman can have a piece. The real mom says, 'No, I'd rather him live and go with the other woman rather than kill him' and the king says, 'Okay, that's the real mom, give her the baby.'"

"That's super dark." Adrian raised his eyebrows.

June laughed. "I know, but that's not the point." She had looked up from staring at her lap to make eye contact with him, and Adrian hoped that was a good sign. "I guess when I suggested splitting my Christmas break in half like this, I figured one of them would go, 'No, that's ridiculous, we're not going to make you fly on Christmas Eve' and let the other one *have me* or whatever for the full holiday." She blew out a breath. "But then neither of them did, so here I am, stuck at the airport on Christmas Eve."

Adrian nodded slowly. "That sucks." Then he gave a short laugh. "Sorry. It's like that's all I can say."

June's lips lifted into a half smile. "No, you're right. It does suck." She ripped the thread off the hem of her shirt. "I mean, traveling on Christmas Eve and all that sucks. But the divorce . . . it's hard, but also, they *never* stopped fighting. Either they were yelling and arguing, or they were silent and passive aggressive toward each other. So when they told me they were splitting up, my first reaction . . . I was sort of relieved. Which is terrible, because who wants their parents to get divorced?" June laughed again, but it was a small, sad, wet-sounding laugh, and Adrian realized tears had started to run down her cheeks.

Without thinking, he put his hand on her shoulder. "I'm sorry. I don't think it's so terrible, though. It sounds like things were really hard on you."

Before he knew what was happening, June was leaning into him, and he had his arm wrapped around her shoulders. It was different than when she'd leaned on him for the photo—her phone wasn't out, her focus wasn't on anything else. He forced himself to remember how to breathe.

She didn't speak for a moment, and Adrian panicked. Was he supposed to say something else? What could he possibly say to make it better? So he just squeezed her shoulder, hoping that she couldn't hear his thundering heartbeat.

After a couple minutes, June sat up again, wiping tears from her face. Adrian let his hand slide off and down to his side. "Sorry. Thank you. Wow, we've known each other for like, an hour, and I'm already crying all over you." She shook her head. "I've never really talked to anybody about that."

Again, Adrian wasn't sure what to do, but before he could respond, June straightened up, like she was resetting herself. "Anyways, what about you? You never told me why you were going to Boston." Adrian hesitated. June gave him a look. "Come on, I just cried in front of you. You can't answer a question?"

He let out a breath. "Okay. We're only in Boston for the holidays with family, then we're flying to Spain."

"Oh cool!" June said, her eyes lighting up. "So you're spending your winter break there?"

Adrian shifted his legs. "Not exactly. We're . . . moving." Ugh. Saying it out loud made it feel real.

June's eyebrows lifted. "Oh?"

Adrian looked at the ground, picking at a loose loop of carpet near his shoe. "Yeah. My dad works for this big international company, and he's always wanted to live in Spain because *his* dad immigrated from there to here way back. So when he had the chance to transfer there, he jumped at it. Even though it means moving all of us in the middle of the school year and my sister is about to graduate high school and none of us even speak Spanish." He blew out a breath. "So, yeah. That's me."

June didn't say anything for a second, her eyes searching his. Finally, she spoke. "That sucks."

Adrian gave her a small smile. "Yeah. You could say that again."

June rubbed her face in her hands. "And you let me go on about how bad *my* life was, while here you are, being dragged halfway across the world!"

Adrian put his hand back on her shoulder, trying not to notice the crackle of energy like electricity when he touched her. "No, come on. Your life still sucks too." June looked up at him, a smile playing on her lips. "Okay, I meant for that to be comforting." He laughed, and then June was laughing with him, and they were laughing together, leaning on each other as they gasped for breath.

June turned her face up toward him, still a little breathless from laughing, her smile wide. He noticed that one eye crinkled closed more than the other when she smiled. Every time Adrian managed to catch a breath, it was full of her coconut shampoo, and the scent scattered his thoughts.

June opened her mouth as if she were going to say something, but then her phone buzzed. She grabbed for it, the giddiness shedding from her frame as tension straightening her shoulders. He saw her swallow. "It's Kaden. Demanding to know who I'm at the airport with." She turned to him. "Well, we know he's seen the picture." She smiled, but it held none of the joy that had filled her face moments before. "Okay, well, what should we do now that we've bared our life stories to each other?"

Adrian's stomach was still doing flips and his heart kept pounding, but this girl was cute and funny and liked Golden Hollow and all he wanted to do was make her laugh like that again so— "If we're really trying to make him believe it . . . we could go on a date? Together?" He tried to keep his voice casual, even as everything in him might crumble if she dismissed the idea.

Her eyebrows shot up. "In the airport?"

Okay, that wasn't a yes, but it wasn't a no. "Yeah. Here. Now. Well, not *now* now, but in maybe an hour? So I can get things set up." Adrian relaxed slightly when she grinned at him.

"Yes! Great idea! Where do I meet you?" Some of her usual bubbliness had returned, and Adrian glowed knowing that he was, at least in part, responsible for that.

"I'm at Gate 14, so let's meet there. One hour. Got it?" He jumped up.

June, grinning, stood as well. "Yes. I'll see you then!"

Adrian smiled at her. He reminded himself that she had only said yes to get rid of her ex, that it didn't mean anything, but somehow the message didn't make it to his stomach, which continued to do flip-flops at the sight of her smile.

5:17 pm

Resa stretched, her arms reaching over the back of the chair. In the hour since they'd sat down, she had pulled her curly hair back into a ponytail, and untucked her shirt. Landry couldn't explain it, but she thought Resa looked even better in this more casual version of her outfit. "Okay. Sitting here has been great, but I need to move."

Landry nodded, trying to gauge if that was a hint that Resa had had fun, but wanted to go do her own thing. She decided to test it. "Want to walk around?"

"Let's do it," Resa said as she stood up. A rush of relief crashed into Landry's chest that Resa hadn't made some excuse to slip away. Resa slipped the strap of her leather bag onto her shoulder as Landry unplugged her phone and stuffed the cord into her backpack.

As they stood on the escalator headed down, a voice came over the announcement system. "All flights from Denver are delayed until 7 pm. If you will miss a connecting flight, please speak to a gate agent, and we will be happy to assist you." Landry and Resa groaned in unison.

"I should text my mom and let her know we're still delayed." Landry pulled out her phone as they stepped off the escalator. Resa walked next to her as she typed.

"Know any other fun places at the airport?" Landry asked with a grin as she locked her phone.

Resa chuckled. "Other than the bar? Nope. I don't spend *that* much time in airports." They walked by a gate, empty save for two teenagers sitting shoulder to shoulder against the window.

"Young love," Landry said in a low voice. "Good luck, kids."

Resa snorted, bumping Landry's shoulder with her own. "We used to be like that."

Before Landry could respond, her phone dinged. She glanced at it, and then her stomach sank. "Oh no."

"What? Is everything okay?" Resa stepped closer, as if she would wrap an arm around Landry.

"No—I mean, yes, no one died or anything. But my mom replied to say that she's bringing my grandma to pick me up, and I just realized I completely forgot to buy her a gift." Landry covered her face with her hand that wasn't holding the phone.

"You forgot to buy your mom a gift?" Resa's eyebrows shot up.

"No, no, of course not. My grandma." Landry groaned as she shoved her phone back in her pocket. "I'm a terrible granddaughter. There goes my title as favorite grandkid."

49

Resa laughed. "Good to know where your priorities are." Landry grinned at her, but before she could respond, Resa looked around them. "Well, where do you want to shop?"

"What?" Landry wrinkled her forehead.

Resa spread her arm out to indicate the shops that they were now walking through. "You need to buy your grandma a Christmas gift, and it looks like your options are limited to . . . " She squinted at the glowing signs around them. "Snax 'N' More, Colorado Limited, or . . . Go Hippy?" Resa frowned. "Maybe not that one."

She turned back to Landry, but Landry didn't follow her gesture to gaze at any of the shops. She was too busy studying Resa.

"What?" Resa asked, nerves clear in her voice as she looked down.

"Are you really gonna help me shop for my nana on Christmas Eve at an airport?" Landry's voice was quiet, muted with affection and disbelief.

"Sure. You can't let Nana down. Otherwise she might write you out of her will." Resa grinned and bumped Landry's shoulder again.

"Can't have that." Landry snorted, trying to calm the fluttering in her stomach. "Well, I guess let's try this Colorado store."

They wandered in to the brightly lit space, empty of all people except for the twentysomething guy working behind the counter. Shelves stacked with souvenirs of all types lined the walls, and Christmas music played through the speakers. The air smelled of overly fake pine scent, as if the store were trying to make up for the fact that they didn't have a Christmas tree.

"So what level of gift are we talking here?" Resa called to Landry as she separated to examine a rack of tchotchkes. "Key chain? Sweatshirt? Shot glass?"

Landry laughed. "Well, she doesn't drive anymore, so no to the key chain. And doesn't drink, so not a shot glass. Sweatshirt isn't a bad idea—she's always complaining about being cold." She flipped through some sweatshirts hanging on a rack. "What about your grandparents? In high school you were super close with them, right?" Landry asked, popping her head up from the other side of the rack to look at Resa, who had moved on to a stack of T-shirts.

"Yeah." Resa swallowed. "My grandma passed away last year."

Landry tilted her head. "I'm sorry. I hadn't heard."

Resa shrugged as she stared at T-shirts in various shades of neon. "It's fine. It's been awhile."

Landry came around to the other side of the rack and placed a hand on Resa's back, just below the nape of her neck. Resa looked at her. "Still. It's hard. I know you two were close."

Resa managed a small smile. "Thanks." She took in a big breath. "Enough about that. What are you gonna get your grandma?"

Landry pulled her hair out of a bun, and then slowly wrapped it up again in another messy knot as she spoke. She was very aware of Resa tracking her every movement and tried to ignore what that did to her core.

"I like the idea of a sweatshirt, but I don't want to guess at her size, and also I'm not sure that she really wears sweatshirts, you know? So I'm thinking a blanket." Landry nodded to a shelf against the wall separated into small cubbies, each containing a rolled-up blanket decorated with a different design.

"That's a good idea." Resa smiled. "I'm sure she'll love it."

"As long as she doesn't find out I bought it in the airport right before going to see her." Landry snorted.

"Still"—Resa caught her eye—"she knows that you're thoughtful and caring."

Landry forced herself to look away. The flutters in her stomach had her thinking like she was in high school again, but she was old enough now to know she and Resa could never work.

She turned and walked quickly to the blankets, trying to ignore Resa's questioning frown. Even as she spoke to Resa, debating the merits of various blanket designs, Landry reminded herself that seeing Resa today didn't mean anything. They were going to hang out for a few hours at the airport, and that would be it. That's all she would let it be.

5:32 pm

Trevor leaned over the counter to look around at the walkway of the airport. Empty. Well, a few people milled about still, pulling their rolling suitcases behind them, but it was basically empty. Nobody who seemed the slightest bit interested in The Slice.

So he slipped around front and trotted across the way to Snax 'N' More. Kat's back was to him as she restocked the candy shelf from a cardboard box open on the ground next to her.

As quietly as his sneakers would allow, Trevor tiptoed up behind her, bent down so he was on her level, and then did his best, and loudest, Santa Claus impression. "HO HO HO!"

The boxes of Junior Mints that had been in Kat's arms clattered to the floor as she jumped and whirled on him. "Are you serious right now?" She swatted at him, and he dodged it, laughing. "You are the worst!"

Trevor had to lean against the other shelf to prop himself up. "You should have seen yourself! You nearly hit your head on the ceiling, you jumped so high." He laughed hard enough that tears started to spring up in his eyes.

Kat bent down to pick up the boxes of candy she had dropped. "You suck, you know that?" She shoved a box onto the shelf so hard that the one behind it started to crumple.

"Aw, you don't mean that." He squatted to help her pick up the boxes.

She tore the box out of his hand and fixed him with a *don't-try-that-again* look. "What do you want?"

Trevor slid his hands in the pockets of his black uniform pants as he stood back up. "Just trying to spread some Christmas cheer." He grinned at her.

Kat rolled her eyes. "Well, now that you've done that, are you leaving?" She faced the shelf again.

"C'mon, don't be mad. It's so slow tonight, I thought we could hang for a little bit till the dinner rush picks up." He bent down so that he was at eye level with her as she knelt to stock the bottom shelves. "Kat?"

She made eye contact with him and shook her head, but he knew her well enough to tell it was a *why-do-I-put-up-with-you* headshake, not an *I'm-serious-get-out* shake.

"Why do I put up with you?" she groaned.

Man, he nailed that.

"Because you love me so much, and I get you free pizza." Trevor stood and shifted so that he was facing Kat, but could also still see the counter of the pizza store in case anybody walked up.

"Not sure about the first part, but I do like the pizza." Finished with the bottom shelf, Kat straightened and put a hand on her hip as she studied him. "Yeah, all right, you can stay."

He snorted, even as his heart seemed to thump louder, like a dog wagging its tail extra hard when you get out food. Why did this always happen around her?

Kat went back to stocking the candy. He thought about how she wasn't dating anyone right now. Maybe this was his chance. Kat was always dating or talking to or hanging out with *somebody*. But not now. Now he had until they left this airport to tell her how he felt.

Maybe.

Trevor chewed on some words, trying to think of something to say, when he glanced at The Slice and noticed someone standing there. "I gotta go, hang on."

"I was gonna let you help me restock though!" Kat called after him as he darted out. He bit back a grin.

Trevor knew his voice was out of breath from his sprint over as he said, "Hello, ma'am, how can I help you?" He really needed to work out more.

The Latina woman had curly hair and was probably in her late twenties. She smiled at him. "Two slices of cheese, please." He nodded and grabbed a triangular box. "So where were you running from? Do you do delivery in the airport?"

Trevor couldn't tell if she was joking. There was a brightness in her eyes, but he wasn't sure if it had anything to do with him. "No, I, um . . . " His eyes trailed across the way to where he could still see Kat restocking.

The woman turned to follow where he was looking, even as Trevor snapped back to sliding the pizza server under a slice.

"I see," she said with a smile, facing him again. "That your girlfriend?"

"Well, um . . . " He trailed off again as he closed the box. Customers were normally in too much of a hurry to make small talk of any kind, much less about his love life.

"Ah," she said in a knowing voice. Then she turned to glance at another woman, with blond hair in a messy bun, who was ordering at the Panda Express across the way. "Let me give you a totally unsolicited piece of love advice, okay?" She handed him her credit card. "If you like her, let her know. She may not like you back, and that will hurt, but it's always worth it. Otherwise you'll regret not telling her how you really feel."

Trevor slid the box of pizza with her credit card on top across the counter. "Um. Yeah. Thanks."

"Merry Christmas." She smiled at him, then walked to stand next to the blond woman, whose face split into a smile when she saw her.

Trevor didn't move for a minute, watching the couple, and then looking back to where he could sometimes see Kat moving around in the store. He swallowed. Tonight. He would tell her tonight.

5:40 pm

Charles had chatted with Ellen and Jon for nearly half an hour, until Sofia declared she needed to go to the bathroom, so Ellen stood up to go with her. After that, Charles flipped through a magazine he'd picked up until his phone started chirping.

He dug it out of the pocket of his slacks and saw his daughter's face smiling out at him from the caller ID. It still jarred him a little bit, even after all these months, when Shonda called him out of the blue like this. Before Angie died, the most he and Shonda had spoken on the phone was when Angie handed him her cell and commanded him to say hello at some point during her hour-long phone calls with Shonda.

"Hi, Shonda," he answered, readjusting how he sat. These chairs felt like they were getting harder the longer he waited in them.

"Hey, Dad," Shonda said. "How are things looking there?"

Charles glanced over his shoulder at the large windows. The snow was still thick enough to blur everything beyond a couple feet into a white mass. "Still snowing."

Shonda blew out a breath. "Sorry you're stuck there." A pause, just long enough to tell Charles what was coming next. "You should have flown out earlier."

Charles let the magazine flop closed. "I wanted to take care of a few things here first."

"You keep saying that, but you won't explain what exactly was so important that you had to wait until Christmas Eve to come see us." A hint of impatience colored Shonda's voice, but Charles decided to ignore it. "Things would be so much easier if you moved here. You'll see when you come. The bedroom you're staying in would be yours permanently, and then I wouldn't worry about you so much."

Charles's mouth twisted into something like a frown. "Couldn't you put that room to better use if you have it? Rent it out to a college student or something and make some extra money?"

He had meant it to be helpful, but when Shonda spoke again, her voice had a bite to it, and he knew he'd said the wrong thing.

"We don't need extra money, Dad. I know you find that hard to believe, but we're doing fine."

Charles did find that hard to believe, but he knew better than to say so. Shonda's husband, Jason, taught history to high school students, which was well enough, but Shonda was a writer—a freelance journalist is what she called it. As far as he could tell, it just meant she didn't have a steady job.

The thought of pushing the point, though, exhausted him today, so he simply said, "I appreciate the offer, but I'm happy where I am. Your mom and I bought this house forty years ago, and I don't plan on leaving it anytime soon." He shifted his legs, and the magazine almost slipped from his lap, so he set it on the chair next to his.

Shonda let out a sigh that was heavy with frustration, one he recognized from the fights they had when she was a teenager. "You keep telling me that." She paused for a moment. "I worry about you, all alone in that house ever since Mom died."

Charles's chest pinched. "I know." His voice softened. "But I'm fine. Really, I am."

There was a crash in the background. He could hear Shonda yelling away from the phone, "Monica! Jax! What was that?" Her voice floated closer to the phone. "Sorry, they're all hyped up because it's Christmas Eve. I should go find out what broke."

Charles chuckled, envisioning the chaos that was waiting for him in Atlanta. "I'll let you go, then."

"Bye. Keep me updated on your flight. Love you."

"Love you, too." He had barely finished the words when Shonda hung up the phone, cutting off her shout at Monica and Jax again.

Charles smiled as he set his phone down on top of the magazine on the seat next to him. He had been dreading this first Christmas without Angie, but it would be good to be around his grandkids and the distracting commotion they brought.

His eyes drifted toward the window as a contemplativeness that had become common since Angela's death set in. Things were so quiet at their house now. Friends still stopped by and filled the silence frequently, but the in-between times were the hardest. The transitioning spaces between waking up and running errands, between dinner and going to bed. Times that used to be filled by Angie's chatter, either to him or on the phone with her friends or Shonda. Now the silent air was heavy, something tangible. Sometimes he felt like it had nestled inside of him, pushing at the space that was hollow after Angie died, trying to widen it. He had taken to leaving the radio on to keep the oppressive quiet at bay.

Still, something in him refused to leave their house. He remembered moving to the area in the '70s, trying to find a house that they liked and could afford as nearly broke newlyweds. When they had seen this house, it was like the stars aligned. There were still pencil marks on the doorway of the kitchen, marking Shonda's growth. Framed photos dotted the walls like a scattered timeline of the family growing and changing. Even though Angie was gone, being in the house was something like preserving her memory, like keeping her close still. Everything inside him recoiled at the idea of a new family moving in, painting over the scuff marks and putting up their own photos and probably knocking down entire walls to make it "open concept."

Charles rubbed a hand over his head, covered in tight-cropped gray hair. Shonda's questions about why he had waited so late to fly out rattled in his head. He wanted to tell her, but he wasn't sure even he had the words to explain.

"Do you wanna read with me?"

A small voice interrupted his thoughts. He looked away from the window to find Sofia standing in front of him with a book in her hands and a wide smile on her face.

"Sofia, leave him alone," Ellen chided, motioning to her daughter. "Come sit."

"No, no." Charles waved a hand. "I'd love to read, if you don't mind."

"You really don't have to," Ellen said, "if she's bothering you." She had a smile on her face that Charles remembered from parenting a young child; one that was a mixture of embarrassment and exasperation but also exhaustion that tempered the other two emotions.

"Not in the slightest." Charles grinned at Sofia and patted the chair next to his. "Hop up."

Sofia clambered onto the chair and opened the book, the wooden covers unwieldy in her small hands. Charles leaned on the armrest separating them to see over her shoulder and read along with her, the silence inside him shrinking a little.

5:46 pm

Kat stepped back from the shelf of candy, satisfied with her restocking job. When her phone buzzed, she grabbed for it, knowing it *had* to be the email. It just had to be.

But as her phone kept buzzing, she realized it was a call coming in, not a notification. She frowned, which turned into a groan when she read her boss's name on the screen.

"Hello?" she answered, crossing her fingers behind her back. *Please don't tell me to stay, please don't tell me to stay.*

"Hi, Kat," Helena said. "Merry Christmas. Listen, I've got a favor to ask you." Helena was nice, but always a bit brusque.

Kat lifted her face toward the ceiling as if that would help her prayers be heard more clearly and squeezed her eyes shut. "Yes?" she asked, straining to keep her voice neutral as she walked back to the front of the store.

"Joanna was supposed to come in after you, but she just called. Her car is caught in a snow drift—it's pretty bad out here. Nearly everyone else is out of town or busy. Since you're already at the store, can you stay and cover Joanna's shift and close up? You'll get overtime on top of holiday pay."

Kat bit back her sigh of frustration. Then she stood on her tiptoes to peek out the sliver of window she could see. The snow was coming down hard. There was a decent chance she'd be stuck here anyways until it lightened up. Might as well make some money.

She forced a smile on her face—she knew that Helena could hear it through the phone—and said, "Of course. No problem."

"Great!" Helena nearly shouted. "Thank you so much. Let me know if you need anything."

"Merry—" Kat started, but Helena had already hung up. " . . . Christmas," she muttered.

Before she could think about what she had signed herself up for, a customer came in. She realized it was the teenager from earlier, who had been reading and then eventually bought a graphic novel. He wandered around the store for a little bit, not really looking at anything.

When he drifted closer to the counter, she raised an eyebrow at him. "Can I help you with anything?"

He looked at her, hope etched into his face. "Actually. Yeah, that would be great, but it's a weird request."

Kat frowned. "Listen, if you try anything—"

"No, no, sorry." The boy had his hands up in a *slow-down* motion. "Not, like, super weird. Just . . . I'm taking this girl on a date. In the airport. Well, sort of a date. It's weird. It needs to be good, but it's harder than I thought. I need some help pulling it off." He ran a hand through his hair as the words tumbled out of his mouth.

Kat studied him for a minute. He wore a graphic tee and looked a little desperate. "The girl you were in here with earlier?"

He nodded, eyes lighting up. "Yeah! It turns out we love this same graphic novel series. She's super cool and cute and she's trying to get her ex off her back, so it's this whole thing, but I need to plan an awesome, Instagrammable date and I really don't want to screw this up."

Kat felt the hopeless romantic inside her go *aw!* She glanced around the store. It was empty, as it had been for most of her shift. And now she was stuck here until eleven. Might as well have some fun.

She nodded. "All right. What do you need?"

6:02 pm

Wes's Twitter feed had started to blur together a while ago. He didn't really care about what any of these people had to say; he just wanted something to do with his hands. He could feel Keely next to him, tension radiating off her like heat off a furnace. But last night had been enough. Wes didn't want to repeat it, especially in a place as public as the airport.

With a groan, he pushed himself off the chair and stretched as he stood. "I'm gonna go to the bathroom," Wes muttered as he shoved his phone in his pocket and started to walk away. He wasn't sure if Keely didn't hear him or didn't want to respond.

A few groups of people wandered around, but the airport was emptier than any Wes had been in before. He guessed that's what happened when you flew on Christmas Eve. The museum where Keely worked was open yesterday, and she'd drawn the short straw and had to work, forcing them to fly to her parents' place today. It was strange to be in the airport when it was this empty, like something out of

The Twilight Zone. Still, he might not hate traveling so much if it could always be like this.

After using the restroom, Wes wandered vaguely in the direction of their gate, but didn't want to actually go sit down again. It was suffocating, fighting with Keely. He couldn't remember a fight worse than this one in the almost five years of their marriage; it was like a physical thing that had a hold on him, weighing his limbs down. Being apart like this lessened it, allowed him to snatch a breath.

He crossed under a large screen advertising an airline that now flew directly to Hawaii, and the terminal opened up into a wider space encircled by shops and restaurants, with the arrival and departure boards in the center. Wes's stomach growled, reminding him that it was close to dinnertime. He examined the slim selection of food, before following his nose toward Panda Express.

As he got in line behind a family, Wes debated whether or not he should see if Keely wanted anything. The petty part of him wanted to show up back at their seats with food and not say a word to her. Wes tilted his head back and forth, tempted, before pulling out his phone.

In line for panda express. Want anything?

He stared up at the menu, trying to remember what he usually ordered here. His mouth watered at the tantalizing smells wafting from behind the counter. In front of him, a family of five was talking loudly, shouting over each other, but it seemed like each person was talking about a different thing. Wes couldn't help but overhear.

"What do I normally get here?" the mom asked, standing on tiptoe to look at the selection of options behind glass.

"We're going on a date and I'll eat then. I'm not going to get anything here, why did you make me come?" the teenage son insisted, arms wide.

"Sofia, do you want rice?" the dad asked the youngest girl, looking forward at the menu.

"Why can't I get pizza?" the older girl asked. "I'm seriously craving pizza right now."

"I like to color." This was said by the youngest girl to Wes. She was at the back of the group and had apparently noticed him listening. Or she was just very outgoing. He thought her name was Sofia.

"Oh—" Wes stuttered. "That's nice. What, um, do you like to color?"

"Cars. David says only boys like cars, but I like cars and I'm a girl, so he must be wrong." As Sofia explained this in a matter-of-fact voice, she spun in a circle, looking down at her shoes, purple snow boots.

Wes smiled. "I think David is wrong too. Is that your brother?" He guessed she was six or seven, and, based on his friends' kids, he thought this was the best age. They were old enough to do some stuff on their own, but still generally thought adults were cool.

Sofia shook her head, still spinning. "No, Adrian is my brother. He doesn't like cars."

"Ah," Wes said, unsure of who David was. Talking with kids who weren't old enough to give a frame of reference was disorienting, but in a way that made him hold back a laugh.

"What do you like to color?" Sofia asked, looking up from her shoes.

"Well, I don't do much coloring," Wes confessed. "I doodle sometimes." He shrugged.

Now Sofia stopped spinning. "What's that?" Her wide eyes stared at him.

"Um." Wes paused. "It's sort of like coloring, but it's . . . smaller? And I usually do it in my notebook, in the side. With a black pen, so there's not really a lot of color."

Sofia wrinkled her nose, clearly repulsed by the idea of coloring with no color, but before she could respond, her dad turned around. "Sofia, do you want—oh, sorry, is she bothering you?" he asked Wes, realizing Sofia had been talking to him.

Wes shook his head, smiling. "No, not at all. Just talking about coloring."

The man laughed a little. "She does love coloring. Okay, Sofia, it's time for us to order." He nodded to Wes, who returned the nod before Sofia and her dad faced forward.

Wes grinned to himself. What would it be like to have a kid who was outgoing and precocious like that? He would have to tell Keely about the little girl—

His thoughts stopped short, like they'd slammed into a brick wall. Right. The fight. They weren't sharing funny stories with each other right now.

With a sigh, he unlocked his phone and saw a reply from Keely.

no thanks

He blew out a breath and faced the front of the line, the weight of their fight feeling heavier than ever.

6:16 pm

June stood in the women's restroom, swishing her bangs one way, then another. Why wouldn't they sit flat? And that one piece kept sticking up. She groaned to the empty room, then ran some water over her hand to try and fix them one last time.

"Why did I pack all my toiletries in my checked luggage," she muttered. Not that she cared what Adrian thought. She wanted her bangs to look good in any photos they took. Obviously.

June glanced at her phone, balanced on a metal shelf attached beneath the mirror. It had been almost an hour since she and Adrian had split up. With one last look in the mirror, she nodded to herself, before setting off to the gate he'd told her to find, carrying her phone and wrist wallet.

When June arrived, any last shreds of confidence she might have had dissipated. Adrian was surrounded by his family. Was she supposed to march up to them and declare she was here for a date—a *fake* date—with their son?

She watched them for a moment, her feet frozen. His little sister was pretty cute. June stood to the side, fiddling with the hem of her T-shirt, debating what to do next, when Adrian glanced up and spotted her. He broke into a big grin, and then nodded to the side.

June smiled back before wandering in the direction he had nodded, until she was standing next to a pillar by the gate. After a minute, she saw Adrian stand up, say something to his family as he shouldered his backpack, then trot toward her.

"Hey!" he said, still smiling as he came closer. "Sorry. My family can be a lot. I kinda figured it would be better if—"

"Adrian, is this your *girlfriend?*" Someone who had Adrian's same dark hair and strong nose sidled up to them, the empty water bottle in her hand apparently forgotten.

Adrian groaned, covering his face with one hand. "Mariel, go away—" Mariel looked like an older sister, June decided. She had that air about her of someone who was used to being in charge.

Mariel smiled at her, but something in her eyes twinkled—June assumed it was at the idea of teasing Adrian. "He won't stop talking about you, you know. The whole past hour he keeps talking about how he has a date—"

"Okay, we're going now!" Adrian interrupted, pushing past Mariel and using his backpack as a shield. "C'mon, June."

"June's a pretty name!" Mariel called after them. "Have fun! Make good choices!" June could hear her laughing as she followed after Adrian.

When they had made it a few yards away, Adrian slowed down and glanced at her. His cheeks were pink again, and she couldn't help but smile.

"Your sister seems nice." June's hand drifted to her bangs, trying to subtly tell if they were cooperating or not. It didn't feel like there were any major pieces sticking up.

Adrian rolled his eyes. "She's always asking about if I'm dating someone. She thinks she's a matchmaker or whatever." They crossed into the section of the terminal with shops and restaurants.

June laughed. "Have you really been talking about me?" She glanced at him, trying to gauge his reaction.

If it was possible, his cheeks grew redder. "Um. Maybe some. Just like, you know, that I have to plan something to help you out." Her stomach did a flip-flop. "Anyways"—he cleared his throat—"are you ready for this?" He began to walk with more purpose, leading her forward.

"Where are you taking me? What should I be ready for?" June raised her eyebrows, quickening her step to keep up.

"It's a surprise. Just follow me."

June didn't ask again, even though her curiosity bubbled up. They walked at a casual pace, passing gate after gate, seeing fewer and fewer people, as they chatted.

Eventually they entered a section at the other end of the terminal that was totally empty and also nearly dark. The sun had already set outside, and the lights in this section of the terminal were shut off. The only light came from the floodlights outside, reflecting the snow and painting everything a muted white hue. Except . . .

June frowned. Up ahead, light flickered against the walls of the terminal. It couldn't be a fire. Maybe an alarm light of some sort?

She glanced to Adrian, who was watching her, his lips lifting into a hesitant smile. "Come on," he said softly.

They reached the strange gate a moment later. "What . . . ?" June couldn't form a sentence.

Strands of Christmas lights draped the rows of chairs, the attendant's counter, and even hung off Command hooks along the window. Everything shimmered and glowed, like they were walking among stars. A blanket was laid out in the center of the space, with paper plates and napkins set up. Slices of pizza steamed on the plates, two cans of soda dripped condensation, and slices of fruit gave a splash of color to the whole setup. There was even a small bouquet of daisies in the center, in what appeared to be a water bottle stripped of its label.

June turned to Adrian, her mouth open. His smile was wider now, but still tentative, waiting for her opinion. His eyes peeked out from behind his curls. "What do you think?"

"This is *amazing*," June managed to say. "You did all this? How did you even find this spot? Did you arrange to have someone turn off all the lights?"

Adrian laughed as he walked closer to the picnic spread, June close behind. "No, I wish I had those connections. I talked to that girl who was working at the store where we met to see if she could help me out. I had thought of a picnic or something, but she told me that this section of the airport gets shut down early on low-travel days so the lights would be off."

They sat down on the blanket, and June ran her hands over the soft fleece fabric. "Did you *pack* all this stuff? In a carry-on?"

Adrian shook his head as he handed her a soda can. "I got it all at airport stores. I don't know why anyone would buy half this stuff at an airport normally, but it worked out for me."

June smiled, taking the soda with one hand and reaching out the other to touch the petals of the flowers. "Daisies are my favorite."

"I figured," Adrian said. June's eyes snapped up from the flowers to him, her brow furrowed.

He cleared his throat, then nodded to her phone, set on the ground beside her. "Your phone case. It's got a pattern of daisies on it." Adrian shrugged, glancing away. "I figured that at the very least you didn't hate them." He finished with a small laugh, clearly trying to play it off, but June couldn't find words. He had noticed and remembered that small detail in just the hour they'd hung out? Kaden had never even brought her flowers, and she was certain he couldn't name what her favorites were.

"Anyways." Adrian gestured to the plate in front of her, with a stack of pizza slices on it. "Dig in." June laughed, and they both picked up a slice.

Thirty minutes later, they had devoured the pizza, guzzled their soda, and even most of the fruit was gone. They had talked throughout the entire dinner: about Golden Hollow, how they'd discovered it, what their schools were like, what they were hoping to get for Christmas.

Adrian finally stood and stretched. "All right. Ready for part two?"

June's eyes widened. "There's *more?*"

"Well, yeah." He grinned, holding out a hand to her. "We haven't even had dessert yet."

June took his hand as she stood up, feeling like her skin was on fire at every point it touched his. She forced herself to let go, and they began walking out of the gate. "What about all this stuff?" she asked, glancing over her shoulder at the abandoned picnic spot.

"I'll come back and clean it up later," Adrian said. "Kat—she's the one who helped me—says no one ever comes through here, so it won't bother anyone."

"Okay." June shrugged. Then she froze. "Wait!" She swallowed. "I, uh, I need a picture."

Something in Adrian's face shifted. "Right. Of course. Where do you want it?"

She led him back to the picnic area and considered it for a moment. "Here—come sit."

June had them both sit down like they had when they were eating, the Christmas lights flickering around them and the makeshift vase of daisies between them. She angled her phone to snap a picture of the daisies, with Adrian in the background. A strand of lights swooped across the corner of the photo behind his slightly-out-of-focus face.

"There," she said, quickly tapping out a caption about her favorite flowers. Her stomach felt like a shaken soda can when she remembered that Adrian had known that. "Okay, good to go."

As they stood, something had shifted. The light, breezy conversation they'd carried all through dinner was now stilted as they walked back toward the other end of the terminal. June chewed on her lip. Technically, nothing had changed. They were still on this fake date to trick Kaden. So why did it feel different?

Adrian cleared his throat as they approached an area of restaurants and shops. "Okay. First, dessert. I have one idea, but tell me if you don't like it."

"I mean, if it's half as good as your first idea, I'm game." She smiled at him and relaxed a little when he returned it.

He nodded to their left. "All right, well, Kat has this friend at the smoothie place, so she hooked us up."

June frowned as they walked toward the kiosk. "For smoothies?"

"Nope. Way better." Adrian smiled at June. "I'll show you."

He led her to a store called Rocky Mountain Juice that had large close-up photos of fruit on the walls and a line of blenders along the back. A twentysomething white girl with strawberry blond hair in a ponytail worked behind the counter.

"Um, hello?" Adrian asked, leaning forward a little bit.

She looked up from her phone at him, shoving the device in her back pocket. "How can I help you?"

"I know Kat." Adrian shifted his weight from foot to foot. "She said you would help us out?"

The girl studied them for a moment. "You're the one on the date?"

Adrian nodded. "That's us."

"Super cute idea. You got the stuff?"

June had no idea what she meant, but Adrian swung off his backpack and dug through it before pulling out a bottle of chocolate milk and hot chocolate packages. He handed it to the girl.

"All right, hang on a sec." She turned around to the back counter and poured the chocolate milk into a large glass container before sticking it in the microwave.

"Okay, so, not smoothies, but I'm still confused." June was standing on her tiptoes to get a better look at what was going on behind the counter as the girl opened a freezer. "What is she making?"

"You'll see," Adrian said, grinning. "I don't want to ruin the surprise." He leaned against the counter, eyes sparkling as he looked at her.

June jumped at a sudden roaring sound, before realizing it was a blender coming to life. The girl pulsed it a few times, then took the glass jar off the base and poured the contents into two plastic cups. She opened a mini-fridge, took out a container of whipped cream, and sprayed it on top of the two drinks.

"Alrighty." The girl picked up the two cups and brought them back to the front counter. "Two frozen hot chocolates, ready to go. Oh, here—" She plucked two spoons from a plastic jar and held them out. "You're good to go."

"This looks delicious." June reached for one of the cups and a spoon. Adrian did the same.

"Thanks," Adrian said to the girl. "This is awesome."

"Merry Christmas." She gave him a little salute before pulling her phone back out.

June spooned up a mouthful. She closed her eyes as she ate it. "Perfection."

Adrian laughed and took a bite. Even he seemed impressed. "Okay, yeah, this is really good. But I've got a place for us to sit and eat it."

June followed him, still scooping up bites of her frozen hot chocolate. After a few minutes, they turned a corner to a part of the terminal she hadn't seen yet. Her eyes widened.

"I found this while I was wandering around looking for a good picnic spot and thought it would be a fun place to hang out." Adrian said it casually as he walked toward a bench, but June suspected it was a bigger deal than that.

Tucked into an alcove along the corridor was a large glass aquarium. June followed Adrian to sit next to him on the bench positioned to allow people to watch the fish swimming inside.

"I never knew this was here," she said before taking another bite of frozen hot chocolate. "What kind of fish are they?" Then she laughed at herself. "I guess you probably don't know that, huh?"

Adrian scoffed. "Sure I do." He pointed his spoon, dripping melted hot chocolate, toward one fish swimming near the bottom of the tank along rocks. "That one is the dangerous Australian Rock Eater." June bit her lip as she smiled. "It swallows rocks from the bottom, then if you try to catch it, it shoots them out at you to defend itself. Sort of a David and Goliath thing." He glanced over at her, a grin tugging at his lips. "Ooh, look at that one." He pointed.

June frowned, following his gesture. "Isn't that a plant?"

Adrian shook his head, face serious except for the laughter glimmering in his eyes. "That's what it wants you

79

to think. It's actually the Leafy Green Shark. It's flat and green and it floats like that, vertical, for most of its life. But if a smaller fish gets close enough, wham! It'll snap out and eat them." He swirled his hot chocolate with the spoon. "It's very dramatic."

June giggled. "I'm surprised they have a shark like that in with the other fish."

Adrian's hand paused, only briefly, as he stirred. "Well, you know, gotta teach kids about the circle of life and all that." He glanced up at June, and when they made eye contact, they both dissolved into laughter.

June managed to catch her breath and set her empty cup on the tile beneath the bench. "Well. Great dessert, and I learned something new about fish, so I'd say it's been a success."

"That's good." Adrian finished the last of his hot chocolate. "You know, just, maybe don't tell anyone else about the fish facts. They may not believe you."

"Got it," June said with a laugh. Her smile softened. "Thank you for this. I'd been nervous about waiting at the airport by myself, especially once the flight got delayed, but this was perfect."

Adrian ran a hand through his curly hair. "Well, good. That's, uh, good."

June caught her lip between her teeth and looked at him. Adrian's eyes flickered from hers to her lips. She was suddenly very aware of how close they were sitting, but she also wanted to be even closer. Their eyes met again.

"Well, look who it is!"

Adrian jumped backward, moving to the farthest edge of the bench before June could blink. She twisted around to see Mariel, Adrian's older sister. She was holding a bag of Chex Mix and looking at them with a glint of laughter in her eyes.

"What are you *doing* here?" Adrian asked. There was an edge to his voice, and June couldn't tell if it was embarrassment or frustration or something else entirely. "Are you following me?"

Mariel rolled her eyes. "Ew, no. *Somebody* didn't get me Chex Mix, and so I figured I'd grab a bag and take a walk, and then happened to run into you two. Don't mind me, I'll keep moving on." She waggled her eyebrows. "Have fun. Not too much fun, though." She sauntered back down the hallway and around the corner.

Adrian rubbed his face in his hands. "Wow. Really sorry about that."

June smiled. "It's okay." She tilted her head at him. What would have happened if his sister hadn't come by? Was she imagining things?

"Do you want to walk around? I'm tired of sitting." Adrian grabbed his trash and stood up.

"Oh," June said, taken aback. Maybe she had been imagining things. She looked at her empty cup. "Guess I should have taken a picture of this before I ate it." June tried to say it with a laugh, but Adrian barely smiled. Chewing on her lip, she quickly snapped a photo, Adrian's hand holding his own cup in the background, and posted it with: **Frozen hot chocolate! Too good to take a photo before it starts melting!**

Right as she was putting her phone away, her phone buzzed. Adrian looked up at the sound, the question plain in his eyes.

June nodded. "From Kaden. 'Seriously, who are you hanging out with?? Call me.'" She snorted. "Yeah, not gonna happen." Locking her phone, she slid it back into her pocket.

She held her breath, expecting Adrian to ask what had happened between her and Kaden. But he just looked at her expectantly. "Ready to go?"

"Yeah." June picked up her cup and followed Adrian away from the bench, feeling like she was standing on ground that wouldn't stop shifting, leaving her constantly off balance.

6:37 pm

"Ooh, this is very you." Landry could hear the mischief in Resa's voice even before she turned and saw the hat she was holding up. They'd finished shopping for Landry's grandma—a blanket with a mountain landscape had been deemed the perfect gift—then ate dinner much earlier than Landry was used to, but Resa insisted her body was still on Atlanta time. Now they were wandering back through the shops, trying to outdo each other with which ridiculous souvenir was available to buy.

The hat in Resa's hands was going to be hard to top. It had a swooping brim wide enough to provide coverage for multiple people, and the blindingly bright yellow material served as the background to the famous C logo from the Colorado flag that was stamped in a pattern around the hat.

Landry shook her head, clucking her tongue. "Sorry. Yellow doesn't work with my hair color. You, however, could pull this off *perfectly*." She grinned.

Resa laughed. "I'll pass for now." She set the hat back on the rack. "Doesn't match anything else I own."

They continued to browse the store, pointing out key chains with kitschy sayings and gaudy Christmas ornaments. Landry couldn't remember the last time she'd laughed this much. Probably with Shelby, at least early in their relationship, right? Landry wasn't sure. She glanced to her left at Resa, who was on her tiptoes, reaching for something on a high shelf with a mischievous look on her face. A small smile slipped to Landry's lips, but she pushed it away. They only had a few hours together until they boarded the plane and Resa returned to her life in Atlanta. Landry was determined to enjoy this short window of time, without ruining it by longing for something else.

Their phones both pinged with notifications simultaneously. They exchanged glances, knowing that probably meant an alert about their flight. Sure enough, Landry's phone glowed with a text announcing their flight had been delayed another hour. Sighing, she returned it to her pocket.

Resa smiled. "Do you know what this reminds me of?" Landry had an idea of what she was going to say, and she covered her face at the memory.

"That choir trip junior year when we got snowed in." Resa crossed her arms in front of her and leaned a hip against the slice of wall next to her. Landry brought her hands down to look at her. "We all thought it was the best thing ever," Resa continued. "An extra day off school and all the chaperones were exhausted, so we practically ran wild."

Landry laughed, shaking her head. "I'd never had so much excitement at an airport."

Resa's eyes glimmered. "Remember what we were all obsessed with drinking during that trip?"

Landry frowned. It hadn't been alcohol—they'd tried to convince various stores to sell to them, with no luck. Some weird soda flavor maybe? "I have no idea," she admitted.

Resa's mouth dropped open. "Seriously? You don't remember?" Landry squeezed an eye closed, trying to think. Finally, Resa spared her. "Chocolate milk with *salt* mixed in."

Landry gasped, clapping a hand over her mouth. "I *do* remember that now!" She laughed. "I can't believe I forgot."

"I can't either," Resa said, laughing. "I don't even remember who suggested it, but that was all we drank for basically the entire trip."

Landry shook her head. "That was so weird. It wasn't even that good."

"Excuse you." Resa unfolded her arms across her chest to point a finger at Landry. "You're misremembering. It was surprisingly delicious."

Landry raised her eyebrows. "For real? Salt in chocolate milk?"

"Yes!" Resa insisted. "You're letting how it sounds color how you remember it tasting. The salt brought out the chocolatey flavor even more. As long as you didn't add too much," she said with a wince.

Landry snorted. "I can't believe you liked it."

The guy working in the store walked by then, carrying a box of T-shirts, and they both nodded to him.

"You would too if you tried it again." Resa put a hand on her hip.

"Don't bet on it."

Landry was grinning, but Resa's smile and voice softened. "That weekend was when I first started to . . . notice you."

"We'd been in choir together for years." Landry tilted her head as she looked at Resa.

Resa waved a hand. "No, I know, but like . . . *really* notice you. You'd been out for a little bit then, and I hadn't come out yet but knew I was gay, and . . . something about traveling together, spending all that time with each other, especially once we were snowed in, it made me look at you in a new light. You know what did it?"

Landry hesitated. Did she want to know? Why was Resa bringing this up? But her traitorous mouth asked, "What?" before she could stop it.

"That last night of the trip—the official trip, before we got snowed in. The chaperones took us to that karaoke joint, and most people were up there in groups, giggling through the songs."

A soft smile pulled at Resa's lips, even as Landry's cheeks heated at the memory she knew Resa was talking about. The reaction to the announcement of the activity had firmly divided the group into excited and mortified. Landry had been in the first camp, but none of her friends wanted to get on stage with her, even though she tried to convince them it was no different than the choir competition they'd just completed.

"And then, out of nowhere, you got up and busted out this spot-on rendition of that Elvis song—'Hound Dog'? I still don't know how you managed to sound so good while also impersonating Elvis, but you totally came out of your shell, strutting around on stage and even going down to dance with random people." Resa shook her head, her smile growing. "I nearly peed myself laughing. I'd never realized how funny you were, but from then on I was paying attention, and suddenly it was clear that you were funny and cool and . . . " She shrugged. "I fell hard."

Landry bit her lip. "I barely remember that." She turned away to play with the strings of a sweatshirt on display, needing something to do with her hands. "I can't believe that was the thing."

Resa shrugged. "What can I tell you?" She glanced sideways at Landry. "Sometimes I wonder what my life would have been like if I hadn't gone on that trip. I almost didn't—I got sick a couple days before, and had to beg my mom to let me go." Landry turned to face her again. "What would have happened if I hadn't gone and never heard you impersonate Elvis and we'd never dated?"

Landry smiled, but didn't respond. Resa continued. "I think senior year would have sucked, for sure. You were the only thing that made it not stressful. And you gave me confidence to actually go after the career I wanted in environmental biology, not med school like my parents expected." She tucked her curls behind one ear. "I guess . . . I guess I'm trying to say thank you. I don't know what will happen after tonight, but . . . I'm glad that I ran into you again."

Resa held Landry's gaze, and Landry swallowed. They were standing so close that Landry could see gold flecks in Resa's brown eyes. Her lungs had apparently forgotten how breathing worked.

And then Resa's phone started ringing.

Resa's eyes broke away from Landry's, toward her phone. "Shoot," she said. "This is the lab. I should answer it."

"Oh, right." Landry didn't know what to make of the aching in her chest. "Yeah, I should actually call my mom and tell her we're delayed again."

"Good idea," Resa said in a tone that suggested she had barely heard Landry. She held her phone up to her ear. "Hello? Jamie? Everything okay?"

Landry stood there for a moment, forcing back the same tears she kept in on so many evenings with Shelby, as her girlfriend had answered emails and phone calls from the office. She forced herself to turn away and leave Resa in the shop, repeating to herself that she didn't care, it didn't mean anything, she had nothing to cry over. She just wished it would feel true.

6:50 pm

Mariel knew she shouldn't. She always knew better, and yet her hand drifted to her phone anyways, her fingers moving as if of their own will as they opened Instagram. Typed in Cole's name. Nothing new.

Letting out a rush of breath, Mariel glanced behind her at the corner she'd turned after running into Adrian and June. She smirked to herself. She really had just been wandering, but the embarrassment on Adrian's face made her wish she'd been prepared to take a photo of it. Still, she was happy for him. She had no clue what his game plan was *after* they left the airport, but she hadn't seen him smiling like that since before they learned they were moving to Spain.

Her thoughts, though, returned to her phone. Instagram was still open. When her mind drifted toward the idea of messaging Cole, she knew she needed backup. She made herself click over to the group DM and tapped out a message.

SOS. I checked Cole's IG for about the fifth time this hour. Someone help me before I accidentally like a pic

Within a few minutes, the other girls in the chat—which they'd nicknamed Girls Who Code—chimed in. There were about ten of them, plus Mariel, and even though they lived all over the world, they'd become some of Mariel's closest friends in the past couple of years.

No!!! Resist! From Nina in Massachusetts, with her sights on MIT next year.

DO NOT GIVE IN. He's SCUM. Candice in England, head of her school's coding club.

He's the one who should be pining over what he's missing out on. He doesn't deserve a second thought from you. Fatima in India, who had gone viral after finding a security flaw in a major tech company's software when she was in ninth grade.

Mariel sighed as she walked past a Cinnabon stand, which she briefly considered stopping at to drown her sorrows. She knew they were right—the group was honest to a fault sometimes. But Cole had unceremoniously ended things barely a week ago. Could anyone blame her if she was still going a little out of her mind?

Her fingers itched, wishing she could pull out her laptop and disappear into a complicated coding problem. That was how she solved all her problems—well, maybe not *solve* as much as *ignore*, but she figured it was better than other coping mechanisms.

She plopped down onto a random chair to finish up her Chex Mix. Her phone buzzed with a notification.

Distraction: Here's a video of Mia!! Liz from Texas sent a video of her dog wearing a Santa hat, and it was enough to make Mariel snort out loud. Her dog was this derpy-looking mutt, and Liz knew how obsessed Mariel was with her.

Thanks, everyone, Mariel sent back.

Also, Coder Grrl has a new YouTube video up if you haven't watched yet!! Candice again.

Mariel had watched it when it came out yesterday, but since she couldn't do any coding herself right now, she might as well disappear into someone else's coding dilemmas. She stood, tossed the empty package into the trash, and pulled up the video as she wandered back to the gate, trying not to think about Cole.

6:58 pm

Trevor swiped through Twitter on his phone. Usually, this time of day he was in the middle of a dinner rush, but with so few people at the airport, things hadn't picked up much. Still, he decided not to head across the walkway to talk to Kat until closer to eight, when he could be certain that most people wouldn't be looking for dinner anymore. Even though there was no one in sight now, he figured he should actually do his job and wait to serve people pizza.

Also, he was scared.

Maybe scared was too strong. But definitely nervous. He wanted to tell Kat how he felt, but what would happen? What if she laughed at him? What if she didn't feel the same way and it ruined their friendship? Trevor groaned and rested his head in his hands. But this might be his one shot. And that other lady had told him to go for it. Surely that was a sign or something?

"You okay?"

Trevor snapped his head up to see Kat standing there, as if he had conjured her with his thoughts. She had

93

an amused look on her face, one eyebrow raised as she peered over the glass guard at him.

"Uh, yeah." He quickly straightened. "You know, tired. Long day."

Kat nodded. "Tell me about it. It's nice not having many people coming through, but also it makes the day go way slower."

"Yeah," Trevor squeaked out, his laugh strained.

Kat frowned. "You sure you're okay? You sound . . . weird." She leaned against the counter.

He tried to smile, but it came out more like a grimace. "Yeah, don't worry about me." Trevor cleared his throat. "Anyways, what's up? You never come over here. It's, like, disrupting the natural order of things."

She rolled her eyes. "I didn't know I wasn't allowed to come say hi when I got bored." Kat turned as if she were going back to the store.

"C'mon, I was just messing," Trevor called. "I didn't know if there was something you needed."

Kat faced him again, smiling. "Not really. Have you seen that kid Adrian come by?"

"The kid who got pizza for his date or whatever?" Trevor asked. Kat nodded. "No, not since he bought the pizza."

"I wanna know how it went. He was so nervous. It was adorable." Kat leaned against the glass and took her phone out to glance at it. Trevor had noticed she'd been checking her phone more than usual lately and he wondered why.

"What're you doing?" Kat asked, eyes glancing up from the screen.

"Trying to fight off this dinner rush." Trevor spread his arms wide to gesture to the empty walkway. "Can't you tell?"

Kat grinned. "And when you're not serving pizza to the masses?"

Trevor shrugged, tracing the edge of his phone. "Nothing much." *Thinking about you.* He swallowed.

"Fascinating." She smiled at him. It was a smile he had seen more times than he could count since they first met in seventh grade. Trevor had moved into her neighborhood, and his first day on the school bus, she had given him that bright smile and invited him to sit next to her. He remembered senior year of high school when she came out as bi to him, and her smile was tentative and uncertain until he pulled her into a hug. He remembered going to her college graduation and how she was unable to contain her smile as she walked across the stage to receive her diploma. Throughout it all, every joke he told, every goofy antic he pulled off, was all to get that smile again.

"Hello? Earth to Trevor?"

Trevor blinked rapidly, and realized Kat was waving a hand in his face. "What?"

"Seriously, what's up?" Kat asked, studying him.

"I . . . " Trevor took a breath. It was now or never.

95

7:03 pm

Landry blew out a long breath. She'd left Resa and that souvenir store nearly fifteen minutes ago, and she still wasn't sure what to think. Had she been imagining that moment between them? She didn't think so, but then Resa was so distracted by her work . . . Landry didn't want to deal with that again.

The plastic-y fake leather of a seat squeaked as Landry sagged into it, tired of wandering the terminal. She remembered that she'd told Resa she was going to call her mom and figured she should actually do that. Her mom picked up after a few rings.

"Hey, Landry-girl! How's the airport?" The warmth in her mom's voice felt like being wrapped in a hug. In the background, Landry could hear Christmas music playing and the sound of laughter from all her extended family that had gathered. She wished she were there right now instead of drowning in emotions at the airport.

Landry rested her chin on her hand, staring out the window. "Still the same. Just got a text that our flight is delayed again. Looking like I won't leave until at least eight." The sun had sunk behind the horizon over an hour ago, and the view outside was a flurry of white snow stark against the black night.

Her mom clucked her tongue. "That's no good. This is why you should never have left the south." Landry could hear the smile in her mom's voice, but wasn't able to return it.

"I know," she said, all too aware that any lightness in her tone was forced. "Hopefully it won't be too late before I can leave, though." She traced the seam on the arm of the chair with her finger, the bumps of the thread cool against her skin.

"Keep us updated." There was a pause, and then her mom spoke. "Are you doing okay, honey? I know things with Shelby ended badly—"

"I'm fine," Landry cut her mom off, squeezing the armrest until her knuckles turned white.

Her mom hesitated before saying, "All right then. As long as you're doing okay. You know, Cora and your cousins offered to come out there and 'teach her a lesson,' if you want to take them up on it."

Landry snorted at the idea of her sister and cousins showing up unannounced at Shelby's place. "Tell them I say thanks."

She could hear the smile in her mom's voice. "I'm sure they'll be thrilled to hear you're considering it."

Landry knew her mom was about to say goodbye, but she wasn't done yet. "Um, Resa's here." She tapped her fingers against the armrest, waiting for her mom's reaction.

Another pause, this one heavy with surprise. "Resa Sanchez? From high school?"

"Yeah." Landry swallowed. Her mom had always been supportive since Landry came out to her, but she didn't know what she actually thought about her first girlfriend.

"Oh, honey, that's lovely!" her mom exclaimed. "How nice you have someone you know there to spend the time with. That actually makes me less worried, knowing you're not alone."

She nodded, the smile on her face more sincere. "Yeah, exactly. It's been nice. I should probably get back to her, actually. Just wanted to check in with you." Landry stood up from the chair.

"Sounds good, honey. Have fun with Resa, and let us know what happens with your flight."

"Will do." Landry hung up and turned back toward where she'd walked away from the souvenir shop. She wasn't entirely sure why she mentioned that Resa was here, only that she wanted to talk to her mom about Resa and gauge her reaction. Not that it mattered if her mom liked Resa. She wouldn't see her again after they left the airport, Landry reminded herself. Still. It was good to know.

7:05 pm

Trevor opened his mouth to tell Kat how he felt. To try and explain to her that he liked her, but if she didn't like him back, it was fine, no hard feelings, but he really was in love with her, so his heart might be crushed. But the words wouldn't come. It was like they had gotten all crammed together in his throat and were now stuck.

Then Kat's phone buzzed on the counter top. She glanced at the notification, and her eyes widened. In her hurry to grab her phone, she almost dropped it.

"What?" Trevor frowned, momentarily distracted. "What's going on?"

"Hang on." Kat didn't look up at him as she tapped on her phone. Her eyes scanned something, and then her mouth dropped open. "I got it! I got it!" she screamed, jumping up and down. She looked at Trevor, hand covering her mouth. "I got it!"

He smiled but couldn't hide his confusion. "Cool? Got what?"

Kat was still jumping. "I didn't want to tell you. I didn't tell anyone, yet. I didn't think there was a chance I would get it." She ran around the counter and threw her arms around him, the lavender scent of her shampoo enveloping him. "But I did!"

He hugged her back, and for a moment, Trevor let himself imagine that this was her reaction to him telling her how he felt. What would it be like if he had said *I love you* a second earlier, and she had jumped in excitement and launched herself over the counter to hug him?

Trevor returned to the present, though, and his confusion. "Kat, I still don't know what you're talking about."

"Okayokayokay," she said in a breathless rush as she let go. "You know I've been writing, but I wanted to get better. So, about a month ago I sort of applied on a whim to this writing fellowship." Kat looked at him, her eyes wide with excitement. "A full year, expenses covered. It's almost like being a writing monk. You live all together and spend the day writing and share the chores and help each other out with critiques and ideas and stuff. It sounded awesome, but I figured there was no way I'd get in. Still, I applied, and . . . " She beamed. "I got accepted!"

Now Trevor almost started jumping. "That's amazing! I can't believe it!" He pulled her into a hug again, not caring about the couple walking by who looked at them with raised eyebrows. "I keep telling you what an amazing writer you are." Something hit him as he released the hug. "Wait—a writing monk? Will I not talk to you for the whole year?" His stomach twisted at the thought.

Kat laughed, still giddy, nearly bouncing on her toes. "No, it's not like that. We can still use the internet and technology and stuff, so we can text and talk all the time, and I'm sure I'll come visit a few times." Time seemed to stop as she said the last part.

"Wait," Trevor said again. "Visit? What do you mean? Where is the program?"

"Didn't I say?" Kat asked. He didn't think it was possible, but her smile grew even wider. "That's the best part! It's in New York City. I'll get to meet a ton of people in publishing, and just *do* so much. Can you imagine having a paid year to live in New York?" She covered her smile with her hands again.

Trevor, though, frowned. "You're . . . moving to New York? For a full year?" He looked down to make sure the sticky tile floor was still beneath him, because his stomach was plunging like a sinkhole had opened up under his feet and sucked him toward the center of the earth.

"Yeah." Kat's eyebrows knit together as she stared at him. "Why don't you sound excited?" She had stopped bouncing.

"Because . . . " Trevor spluttered. "That's far away. And it's a long time."

"It's not *that* long." Kat shrugged. "Only a year. Although wouldn't it be great if I ended up living there after? I've been saving up, so I could have a few months of rent paid for, then I could get a job somewhere and write in the evenings." Her eyes brightened again, but Trevor didn't feel like she was looking at him anymore, lost in her imagination. "Or maybe I'll come out of the program with a book good enough to pitch, and I'll get an agent and a huge advance payment and use that . . . ."

"You can't move to *New York*," Trevor interrupted.

Kat's gaze returned to him as she crossed her arms in front of her chest. "Why not?"

"Be*cause!*" Trevor flailed his hands around, as if he could pull the right words from the air. "You just *can't*. It's too far."

Kat rolled her eyes. "Okay? People move far away from their hometowns all the time."

Trevor leaned against the counter. It felt like the world had been abruptly mirrored in reverse. Like something was deeply wrong, but no one else either noticed or cared. How could Kat leave him like this? "We've known each other since middle school. You can't leave. You can't live in New York. You're . . . *you*."

Kat frowned, her shoulders tensing like they did whenever she felt threatened. "What does *that* mean?"

Trevor ran a hand through his hair. He could read her well enough to know she was frustrated with him, but he felt like he was trying to hold a fistful of water that kept spilling out of his grasp. "You know! We always talk about doing big things, but I didn't think you'd ever actually leave Denver." What he meant but didn't say was *I didn't think you'd ever leave me.*

"I didn't ask you for permission," she snapped, anger flashing in her eyes. "I don't *need* your permission, actually. I told you about this because I thought you would be excited for me, not try to talk me out of it or insist that I can't be anything more in life."

"Kat, I—"

She turned to leave, boots tapping on the tile. "Just because *your* only ambition is to work at some airport pizza place doesn't mean that the rest of us can't have dreams."

Kat walked back to the store, but Trevor couldn't move. Is that really what she believed about him? That all he wanted was to work here for the rest of his life? Didn't she know him better than that?

Trevor swallowed. Part of him wanted to run across to the store, to explain everything, to tell her he had said all that because he loved her, not because he was a jerk. But something else kept him rooted to where he stood. If she thought so little of him, maybe he was better off without her. Maybe he had been wrong about her all along.

7:23 pm

Mariel traced her fingers over the spines of books on the shelf. The airport version of the Tattered Cover bookstore wasn't as extensive as the locations she usually visited, but it still filled Mariel with a shimmering warmth to be among books. After a quick glance around to make sure no one was nearby, she closed her eyes and breathed deeply. It even smelled like a normal bookstore, as if by stepping into the shop she had been transported to a haven away from airports and frustrated passengers and bad fast food.

Opening her eyes, Mariel let out the breath in a sigh. Books had been her escape since she had first learned to read. Yes, she loved coding and could lose herself for hours on the computer. But when she emerged, eyes aching from staring at the glowing screen, books were a welcome reprieve, something she didn't feel the need to *solve*, only to enjoy.

"Looking for a certain book? Or just browsing?" said a voice behind her.

Mariel turned, expecting to see an employee smiling at her, but was surprised to see an older white man. She realized he was the man Sofia had been talking to earlier and smiled politely. "Mostly browsing. But I usually come in to look around and then end up buying something, so I guess we'll see." There was that one fantasy book she had been eying . . .

The man returned her smile in a way that said he understood. "You're . . . Mariel, right? Sofia's older sister?" Mariel nodded. "I'm Charles." He held out his hand, and she shook it. Then Charles gazed at the bookshelf behind her, which was taller than her head. "I'm just looking too. Books have always brought me comfort."

"Same." Mariel looked at the shelves around them. "That's really why I came in here. I wanted to escape, for a little while."

Charles studied her, considering his next question. "Sofia mentioned you're moving. Are you doing okay?"

Something in Mariel's chest seized, even though the fact that they were leaving the U.S. had been set for months. It was like every time someone mentioned it, the pain cut through fresh. She swallowed. "Yeah. My dad's job is moving us to Spain. In the middle of the school year. So we'll spend some time with family in Boston, then . . . we'll be gone." She chewed on the inside of her lip.

Charles's nod was slow and heavy. "I'm sorry. That can't be easy."

Mariel's throat tightened, but she tried to hide the emotion with a shrug. "Yeah. But next year I'll graduate high school and can come back here for college." She glanced at the floor.

When she looked up, Charles was watching her, his eyes gentle. "High school is hard enough without having to move to a new country in the middle of it," he said, tilting his head.

The tears that Mariel had managed to hold back until now forced their way forward. She nodded, swiping at her eyes. "I know it's just the last year and a half, but that's such a long time. And everyone at whatever school I go to will already have their friends, you know? By junior year, everything is set. I have friends here, and a boyfriend—well, I *had* a boyfriend here, till he broke up with me because he didn't want to be long distance. I'll be the new girl, and I don't even speak Spanish. Who's gonna want to hang out with me?" She gulped down a breath and managed to stem her tears. She was fine. It was all fine.

Charles gestured to a wooden bench positioned against a wall. "My knees aren't what they used to be. Sit with me?" Mariel nodded, and they lowered themselves onto the bench. Mariel tucked one leg up under her. "Have you talked to anyone else about this?" Charles asked.

Mariel shook her head. "Not really. I tried telling my friends here, and they're sad I'm leaving, but they don't get it." Even her friends in the Girls Who Code group chat had only been able to offer meager amounts of comfort, mainly focused on how she would be close enough to easily visit some of them.

"And my parents . . . they've already got enough going on. They're stressed all the time." Mariel fiddled with the zipper of her boots. "My dad is so excited, he doesn't want to hear about what any of us thinks. And Mom is excited too. They've been talking about living in Spain since they first got married or whatever. And she's swamped trying to keep everything organized and figuring out what it means to move to a new country. I don't want to be another thing for them to worry about." She kept her eyes on her boots.

"I understand," Charles said. He leaned back against the wall and settled his hands in his lap. "But as a parent, I can promise you that they'd want to know how you feel. They may not be able to do anything to fix it, but we always want to know if you're struggling with something."

Mariel shrugged, glancing up at him. "I guess."

They were quiet for a moment. Charles seemed to be thinking about something, and Mariel was wondering if she should tell her parents how she felt. But they were already so busy taking care of Adrian and Sofia—did she want to add to that? Shouldn't she be helping them instead of making things harder?

"Mariel." Something in Charles's voice was more serious, and it made her look up at him. He held her gaze. "Will you promise me? Tell them how you're feeling. I think you'll feel better, and I know they'll appreciate it." Mariel

107

hesitated, and Charles continued, leaning forward a little bit. "My daughter and I . . . we never really got along. She was always closer with her mother, but she and I struggled to see eye to eye. Now her mom is gone, and I'm trying to make things right, but I'm worried she won't tell me how she's doing." He looked away at the shelf in front of them. "So I know that even if it seems like your parents don't have time or don't care, they do. They're already worried about you. It's what parents do. But they'll be less worried if you're honest with them, instead of trying to be brave." His gaze returned to Mariel.

She pressed her lips together, then nodded. "Okay." Charles smiled at her, and she smiled back. "Do you have grandkids?" She appreciated Charles's advice, but she was also sick of talking about moving—it felt like that's all she had done for months.

This was clearly a question Charles loved. "Two." He reached into the pocket of his slacks to pull out his phone. "Monica is about your sister's age, and Jax is four. They're a handful, to say the least." He chuckled as he angled his phone to show her pictures.

"Do you live near them?" Mariel asked, looking at the photo of two kids with light blond hair, their faces smeared with what looked to be red popsicle.

Charles shook his head. "I live here in Denver, and they're in Atlanta. Shonda wants me to move in with her, but I don't want to leave my home." He paused. "My wife,

Angie, and I bought it right after we were married. It's where we raised Shonda and made all our memories."

Mariel chewed on her lip. "And your wife . . . she passed away, right?"

Charles didn't answer for a moment, and Mariel kept looking at the photo of his grandkids to give him space. Finally, he spoke. "Yes. In February. That's why Shonda wants me to move in with them. She doesn't like the idea of me being alone." He gave a thin laugh. "But it's hard to leave a house that's so full of Angie. It would be like . . . " Charles paused, then cleared his throat. "Like saying goodbye to her all over again."

"That's hard." She hesitated, then said, "I obviously don't know what it's like to have a wife die, but I know what it's like to have to say goodbye to a home. It's not fun. I hope you don't have to say goodbye to yours."

Charles smiled at her. "Thanks."

Before either of them could say anything else, Charles's phone, still in his hand, dinged. Mariel felt hers vibrate in her pocket. They exchanged a glance, and then Charles clicked on the incoming text.

All flights out of Denver on 12/24 have been canceled. Please see your gate agent for more information.

Mariel groaned, slumping against the wall behind the bench. "Oh no. Are we gonna be stuck here for Christmas?"

"Might be," Charles said. "The snow is coming down pretty hard outside. I don't think anyone's going to be driving in that."

"I should probably go find my parents." Mariel stood up. "It was really nice talking to you."

Charles nodded. "The pleasure was all mine. I'm sure we'll see more of each other, but until then, merry Christmas."

"Merry Christmas." Mariel smiled, then went to find her family, her steps a little lighter than earlier.

7:49 pm

When the text buzzed through on Keely's phone announcing their flight had been canceled, Wes reacted to his own text before she even had time to process the news. He tensed up next to her, as if he were undergoing rigor mortis in a matter of seconds.

Then Wes stood up, his bad knee popping from the force of the movement loudly enough for her to hear it. "I'm going to go stretch my legs. Looks like we'll be here for a while."

Keely frowned, before standing up too. "I want to walk with you."

She watched the debate in his head as it played out across his face. He clearly didn't want her to come, but he also didn't want to start a fight over it. Finally, he nodded and turned away without saying anything. She followed.

They walked in silence for a few minutes, the only sound that of their shoes on the tile floor and the subdued bustle of an empty airport—the whirring of the moving walkway, plates clattering in a restaurant kitchen.

Keely blew out a breath as they passed by the escalators. "So that's it? We're spending the night here?"

"Guess so." He didn't look at her. "There's a hotel connected to the airport. I can call and see if they have any rooms, but I overheard some other people saying they're full, so I'm not hopeful." Wes's pace had picked up from a casual stroll to an intense, directed pace that was almost a jog.

"Are you going somewhere?" Keely asked, quickening her steps to keep up.

"No, I just wanted to walk." His gait didn't slow.

"Well, you're not walking, you're nearly running. I feel like I'm training for the Olympic speed-walking event."

"I don't think that's a thing."

"It is too a thing," Keely insisted, jogging a few steps to reach his side as they made their way past several nearly empty gates. "And even if it's not, you know what I mean. You're going fast."

Wes slowed his pace marginally. "You didn't have to come."

"I think we should talk about this." Keely pushed the sleeves of her sweatshirt up to her elbows.

"I think you did plenty of talking last night." Wes's voice was as dark as a storm cloud.

"*I* did plenty of talking?" Keely's voice pitched upward in disbelief. She hated how it did that, how incredulous anger made her sound weak. "You did plenty yourself."

112

Wes was shaking his head. "Stop it. Not here. We're in public."

Keely stopped walking and spread her arms out wide, gesturing to the empty chairs surrounding them. "*Nobody* is here. You're just looking for an excuse to avoid this discussion, but we have to have it."

Wes paused a few feet ahead of her. "I thought we were waiting until after Christmas to talk about it."

"No, that's what *you* declared last night, when *you* decided *you* were done with the conversation." Keely now folded her arms. "I wasn't going to push it, but now we're stuck here together, so we might as well. I don't want my mom to pick up on any tension between us."

Wes ran a hand through his hair and mumbled under his breath, "This is why we should have gone to my parents' for Christmas."

Keely let out a barking laugh. "Really? You're gonna bring that up now?" She actually liked going to Wes's family for Christmas—his grandparents had immigrated here from the Philippines, and his whole family still celebrated using Filipino traditions. Staying up till midnight celebrating was certainly more fun than her parents who went to bed at 10 pm. But that wasn't the *point*.

He let out an exasperated breath. "Why not get all the arguments out, right? If you're gonna insist we talk about this one."

"I don't *want* to argue. I want to talk about this like adults, and it has to happen soon because they want an answer by New Year's." She tried to keep her voice calm, but even to her it sounded thin and brittle.

Wes groaned. "What kind of people work there that they want an answer over the holidays?"

"Stop changing the subject," Keely snapped. "That's not the point."

"I think it's part of it, though." Wes shoved one hand into the pocket of his pants. "Company culture."

Keely rolled her eyes. "It's a museum. They're open the week between Christmas and New Year's, so people have to work, so it's normal to hear from other museum people during that time. And besides, it's competitive. There are dozens of other people who would take it, so they don't need to waste time giving me time to think about it. I think she was shocked when I asked for a week to think about it." Keely raised an eyebrow meaningfully. "Most people would have said yes immediately."

Wes threw up his hands. "Really? Most people would have agreed to move from Arizona to Oxford, England, without a second thought?"

Keely rubbed her face. "Well, normally we would have talked about the possibility before the job offer, and decided to either say yes or no if they offered. But *you* refused to even talk about it."

"You said you only applied to make your friend there happy!" Wes pointed at her. "You said there was no chance of them offering you the job, and you wouldn't move there anyways. I figured it was some weird way of challenging yourself."

"I *never* said I wouldn't move there." Keely took a step forward. "I didn't think I would get the job, sure, but I always knew that if they offered it to me, I'd move there in a heartbeat. It's the Ashmolean! It's been my favorite museum since we visited in college. Did you really think I wouldn't want the job?"

"I thought you'd be happy enough with what we have to at least *consider* saying no." Wes spat the words out like they were venomous barbs aimed at her. "I didn't realize you were so unhappy with your life that you needed to upend everything and move halfway across the world."

"That's not what I'm doing, and you know it," Keely said. "I was happy in Arizona. I still am. But this job . . . even if it's just an assistant collections manager position, at this museum, it's the opportunity of a lifetime. It's not about how I feel about where I've been. It's about where I want to go."

Wes groaned, turning away from her. "Can't you hear yourself? You're so wrapped up in what this means for *you* that you never stopped to think about *us*, about our marriage, about our future family."

Keely froze. "What do you mean, 'our future family'?"

Wes blinked, twisting to face her again. "What? Nothing."

Everything started to make sense. This was about far more than her taking a new job. "It's not nothing. What did you mean," she repeated, but it was less of a question and more of a command.

Wes ran a hand through his dark hair. "Fine. Do you remember that right before you got the call, I had told you there was something I wanted to talk about?"

Kelly chewed the inside of her cheek. It sounded vaguely familiar, but that whole night was a blur in her memory now—from the excitement of getting the job to the crushing realization that Wes wasn't happy for her to the heated yelling.

"I figured you didn't." Wes shrugged. "A lot happened that night, and I didn't bring it up again. But the thing that I wanted to talk to you about . . . it was about trying to have a kid. It had been on my mind for a while."

He paused, letting that sink in. "So I had mentally prepared myself for that conversation, and then you announced you'd gotten the job. That's why my reaction wasn't immediate excitement. I was so caught off guard, and I thought it meant we couldn't have kids anytime soon. I was disappointed, but not about your job."

Keely was silent for a long moment, digesting all of this information. Eventually she spoke. "You want to have kids." Wes nodded. She bit her lip. "But we said before we got married that neither of us wanted kids."

She saw something dim in Wes's eyes. Knowing she caused that felt like being dunked in ice water, but what she had said was true. She had never particularly wanted kids, even in her late twenties when all her friends were going baby crazy. She was perfectly happy to hold someone else's kid until it started crying and then hand it back. When she and Wes were getting serious, she'd been relieved to hear he felt the same way. But now . . . he'd changed his mind?

Wes had been quiet for a moment, but now he spoke. "I know. But that was almost five years ago. I've changed a lot since then, and so have you. I thought maybe you'd changed your mind about this."

Keely pressed her lips together. "I don't know why you would think that. That's a *big* change to assume about me."

Wes frowned. "You won't even consider it?"

"I don't know . . . " Keely pulled the sleeves of her sweatshirt back down. "I'm not saying that. I haven't really thought about it since we got married. But I didn't think it was a conversation that was open, because we'd already *had* it."

The fluorescent lights buzzed overhead as Keely waited for Wes to answer. "I know. I guess I'm saying I'd like to reopen it." He looked at her. "Can we do that?"

Keely studied Wes's face. Hope was etched into every feature. She swallowed. "I . . . I could if nothing else were changing. But there's still this job offer. I still want to move to Oxford. I want *us* to move to Oxford. I don't know . . . " She chewed her lip.

"But we can do both." Wes stepped toward her, his words coming fast now. "I've been thinking about it, and I know my initial response was to assume that we couldn't have kids in England, but people do that all the time! I mean, having kids in a different country. Not just having kids in England. Although they do that too." He laughed a little, but Keely could tell it was nervous. "You can take this job, and once we've settled in, we can start trying."

Keely was shaking her head though. "But that's not the problem. I don't know if I even *want* kids. No matter where we're living."

Wes's shoulders slumped. "We can't even talk about it?"

Keely felt the same way she had as a kid when she first saw one of those optical illusions, the kind that looks like a duck so clearly, until all of a sudden your brain switches and you're looking at a rabbit. Like she had thought she knew who Wes was and what their marriage was like, but now she couldn't trust her own senses.

"I—I don't know." She took a step back. "But I can't have this conversation right now."

Wes's face turned stony. "So you're gonna decide that the conversation is over."

Tears sprang to Keely's eyes at his tone, but she tried to keep her voice steady. "I'm just saying that this was *a lot* and it's not what I expected, and so I need some time to myself, okay?"

"Fine." His voice was hard. "No one's stopping you, then."

Keely turned away, her tight throat making it difficult to swallow. Her steps echoed in the empty terminal, and she kept hoping for Wes to follow her or call after her, but he never did.

8:12 pm

The window, washed white by the snow outside, showed faded reflections of Resa and Landry as they walked. Resa was on the phone with the hotel attached to the airport. Landry watched their reflections and imagined they were images of their past selves, ghosts once forgotten that had now been resurrected. The thought unsettled her, and she looked away from the window.

After talking with her mom, Landry had found Resa waiting at the gate for Atlanta. The smile on Resa's face when she'd seen Landry sent sparks through her veins. They'd sat and talked for a while, and then after the announcement that all flights were canceled, decided to stretch their legs.

Resa sighed as she hung up. "No luck. Apparently everyone else thought about getting a room before we did." She slid her phone into her pocket.

"Sounds like we're staying the night at the airport," Landry said. She waited to feel devastated at the idea of spending Christmas Eve in the airport, but found that, while she was disappointed, she also didn't mind the idea of having more time to spend with Resa. Landry swallowed, not sure that was a good thing.

"Seems so." Resa turned to Landry, a smile playing at her lips. "In that case, I have a surprise for you."

Landry's eyebrows shot up. "Okay . . . ?"

"Follow me." Resa marched forward, leaving Landry with no choice but to trail along behind her.

After a few minutes of walking, they reached a cluster of tables in a secluded area of the airport. Oversized abstract sculptures hung from the ceiling—rectangles of various sizes and colors, like strokes of paint suspended in the air.

"What is this?" Landry asked, turning to Resa.

She smiled. "I picked up some stuff while you were talking to your mom and figured we could have a little fun since we're stuck at the airport. C'mon."

Landry followed Resa to the table and sat down. Resa reached into her leather bag and pulled out a few items, keeping them hidden until she placed them on the table.

Landry groaned, even as she smiled. "You're not serious."

Sitting on the table before them were two bottles of chocolate milk and a handful of salt packets.

"Deadly serious." Resa smirked. "Just try it, and if you hate it, I'll never mention it again."

Landry shook her head as she reached for a bottle. "Fine, you weirdo."

Resa laughed, clapping her hands together. "Get ready to eat your words."

They cracked open the seals on the bottles, but Landry handed hers back to Resa, who mixed the salt into the milk, pouring and shaking and sipping. Landry wondered if the concentrated look Resa wore on her face was something similar to how she looked in the lab.

After a few minutes, Resa set down a bottle with a satisfied sigh. "There. Perfect."

She slid a bottle to Landry and picked up the one in front of her. "Bon appetit." Landry hesitated, eying the bottle in front of her. "C'mon," Resa urged. "On the count of three. One, two, three!"

Resa tilted her bottle into her mouth, and after a second's hesitation, Landry did the same. The cold milk flowed into her mouth, and Landry's eyes widened.

It was *delicious*. The salt faded to the background, and the chocolate flavor popped, far better than any store-bought chocolate milk she'd ever tried. It was like drinking sea salt chocolate.

As Landry set the bottle back down, Resa was waiting, a smile on her lips. Landry sighed. "Okay. You were right."

"Yes!" Resa pumped a fist into the air. "I *told* you!"

"It doesn't make any sense!" Landry picked up the chocolate milk as if to study it. "It sounds terrible."

"Yeah, so does *every* unknown good snack combo." Resa took another sip. "But then you try it, and, inexplicably, it works."

Landry drank more. "Okay, okay. I'm sorry I doubted you."

They laughed and chatted for a bit, until they had both drained the milk in their bottles. It really was like that trip in high school, Landry thought. Stuck at the airport, just enjoying being with each other. Tension slipped out of her shoulders. It was fun being around Resa, and she was able to be herself in a way she hadn't felt comfortable doing in a while.

There was a lull in the conversation, and Resa looked out of the large window to their right, the outside still smeared in gusty white. "Does it snow like this often?"

Landry followed her gaze. "I mean, it snows a lot. But this is a full-on blizzard. They're not as common. Usually the sun comes out the next day and melts most of it away, and after a couple days you wouldn't even know it snowed."

"Huh." Resa was still looking out the window. "Do you drive in the snow? I'm guessing it's not like Atlanta where everything shuts down at the first sign of a flurry."

Landry chuckled. "Definitely not. Otherwise we wouldn't work half the year. If it's really icy, they'll close stuff, or people work from home if they can. But usually you just suck it up." She propped her chin on her hand. "Snow is way less exciting when you're shoveling twelve inches of it off your car instead of watching it fall from inside your home, curled up with coffee and a fuzzy blanket."

She smiled at Resa, but Resa was wrapped up in her thoughts. "Any reason you're asking?" Landry prodded.

This snapped Resa out of her daydream. "What? Oh, no. Just curious what it's like to live somewhere that snows. That's all." She turned away from the window and began messing with something in her bag.

Landry frowned. It didn't seem like that was all. "Sucks though. I'm sure you're ready to get home." Resa made a noncommittal noise. Landry chewed on her lip, before speaking. "I don't think you ever actually told me why you were in Denver."

Resa stopped what she was doing with her bag and straightened to face Landry. She looked down at the table, twisting the empty bottle in her hands. "I . . . " She blew out a breath. "Okay. I'm not supposed to tell anybody because it's not official and they haven't announced it yet, but I applied for a position at the University of Colorado in Boulder a while back, and this week was my final interview. And . . . I got it." She met Landry's gaze. "I'm moving to Colorado." Landry didn't speak.

"But like I said, it hasn't been announced yet," Resa continued. "My family doesn't even know. So, don't say anything, I guess, if you see them." Resa was beaming. She pressed her hands to her mouth. "You're the first person I've told. It makes it feel so much more *real*, you know, saying it out loud. I'm teaching at the university. I'm moving to Boulder!" The last bit came out as more of a squeal.

"That's great!" The cheeriness in Landry's voice was forced, and she knew Resa noticed. But all the happiness she'd felt moments ago, the same contentedness she had in high school that had infused their time together tonight—it was gone, melted like snow in the afternoon sun. Reality came crashing back in as she saw the two of them from an outside perspective: Resa was at the top of her career, moving across the country to teach at a prestigious university. Landry was struggling to make her bakery work. And hadn't Resa herself said that her career was the reason why no relationship she was in had ever worked out?

"Landry?" Resa leaned closer to her, concern filling her eyes. "What's up?"

"Oh, um, nothing. I'm really happy for you." Landry made her lips turn into a smile. She could fake it at least until they left the airport. Then she would figure out what to do later. Nothing had to change.

But it seemed Resa had a different idea. Tentatively, she reached a hand across the table and placed it on one of Landry's. Her breath caught at the touch of Resa's hand on hers. "I should have told you sooner. I don't know what you're thinking, or what you've been thinking all of tonight, but to me . . . " She smiled, and it was so soft and tender that Landry's chest squeezed. "To me, it means we can have another chance to make this work. To make us work. I'd like to try, if you do."

For a moment, the entire world around Landry froze. Even though it had been ten years since they broke up, Landry had occasionally imagined *what if* about the two of them. And here they were, with a chance to try again. Her stubborn heart lurched, and the word *yes* almost slipped from her mouth.

But her brain intervened. She'd been down this road before, and she knew how it would turn out. She and Resa would start dating, and at first it would be great. Landry would be so proud of all of Resa's achievements, and Resa would even pretend to be proud of Landry's bakery. But then Resa would get bored, slowly realizing she deserved someone better than Landry, but too nice to say anything, until she couldn't *not* say something and it all came bursting out in a horrible fight. It was what had happened with Shelby. Landry knew in her bones it was what would happen with Resa.

So she pulled her hand back and dropped it into her lap. Resa seemed to shrink in on herself as she swallowed hard. "Landry . . . "

"I'm sorry." Landry pushed her chair away from the table. "I'm so sorry. We wouldn't work. Maybe you don't see that now, but you will, eventually. I really am excited for you and your new job and your new life, but I can't be a part of it. I'm sorry."

"Landry, wait—" Resa stood up.

But Landry was already turning away from the table, from Resa, from the window reflections of their younger selves.

8:23 pm

They were spending the night at the airport. Mariel figured that lined up with how the rest of her year had gone. The rooms at the attached hotel were exorbitantly priced and, from the conversations around them, sold out anyways. No way to drive home in this either. Although Mariel laughed at herself—drive home. Where was home anymore?

"But what about Christmas?" Sofia kept asking. "And Santa? Will he know we're here?"

"Shh, yes, it will be fine," Mom said, trying to distract her with the iPad. "Think of this as a fun adventure."

Sofia was only partially satisfied with this answer. Mariel wished she knew how to help make things better. She hated being so helpless—with her family, her relationship, her *life*. She wanted to *do something*.

"I'm gonna go for a walk," Mariel said to no one in particular. Her mom nodded to her, still focused on Sofia, and she pushed up off the chair.

Wandering through the airport, Mariel's mind couldn't stop racing with everything that had gone wrong in the past couple months. Everything that had happened *to* her. Her dad's new job. Cole breaking up with her. Now their flight that she didn't want to take in the first place was canceled, and on Christmas Eve. She ground her teeth, and even though she knew it wouldn't help, she opened Instagram.

No new photos on Cole's feed or Stories. Sighing, she swiped through Stories from other people she knew. Most of them were of the snow or Christmas Eve celebrations. Then she gasped, coming to a sudden halt. It was a photo of Cole, but not on his account.

It was a selfie photo of Cole—his dark brown hair that curled around his ears, his wide, infectious grin. And . . . Kennedy? Who she'd hung out with nearly all of high school? They weren't that close, but they'd run in the same circles enough that Mariel had considered her a friend. Close enough to know that Kennedy had always had a crush on Cole, and to notice how Kennedy disappeared from her life once she and Cole had started dating last summer.

Mariel's breath caught in her throat as she studied the photo. Cole, grinning with his arm wrapped around Kennedy's shoulders as she leaned into him, a hand placed protectively on his chest. Kennedy had captioned the photo *Miss having my man to keep me warm!!* with a kissy face emoji.

129

Mariel wanted to throw her phone across the airport. She and Cole had been broken up for a *week* and he'd already moved on? Maybe, she realized with a sinking feeling in her gut, he'd been over her for a long time and hadn't quite gotten around to dumping her. Her face heated. She sent the photo to the Girls Who Code group, not bothering to write an explanation.

Immediately the group filled with gratifying outrage.

IT'S BEEN ONE WEEK!!

What a loser!

You're better off without him.

Even still, Mariel's mind wouldn't stop whirring. She thought of Charles's advice to talk to her parents. She considered it for a moment, she really did. But this wasn't about moving. This was about Cole. Her parents didn't want to hear about that. And no matter what Charles said, they were already so busy. She didn't want them to worry about her any more than they already were. It had always been her job as the oldest to be the strong one and help take care of Adrian and Sofia. Now, with everything going on, was not exactly a great time to stop doing that.

So Mariel took a deep breath and kept walking, forcing one foot in front of the other. She needed something to do, something to keep her occupied, or she was going to lose her mind. Or worse, call Cole and yell until she cried. She needed a problem to solve.

And then, like an answer from the heavens, she stumbled across a shop full of discounted Christmas decorations. Inspiration sparked in her mind. One problem she had was with Cole, yes, but there was no good way to fix that. Another one, though, was that they were going to have Christmas in an airport. She couldn't fix that entirely, but she could at least make the best of it.

Now her mind was spinning, but with ideas as she studied the displays in the store. They could decorate the gate and invite everyone else stuck at the airport as well. They could count down to Christmas like it was New Year's Eve. It would be a special surprise for Sofia, but maybe also for her parents, something to let them relax and enjoy. It would be a huge party, with lots of details to organize: food, decorations, somehow inviting everybody, presents for Sofia. Lots to focus on and figure out in—Mariel checked the time on her phone—three hours and forty-nine minutes.

She could feel her blood thrumming in her veins, something similar to the thrill she got when she stumbled upon a new solution to the coding problem she was trying to solve. A sense of purpose, something to aim for. She grinned, and took out her phone to make a list—the first step in anything that required planning. As Mariel walked and typed, her footsteps were confident, filled with purpose. Maybe she could turn this around after all.

8:31 pm

In the past hour, Trevor had seen Kat walk past the entrance of the shop three times, all without so much as a glance toward him. That was fine by him. She owed him an apology as much as he owed her one.

Still, though, he couldn't help but look at the store every few minutes, hoping to make eye contact with Kat, or maybe even to see her walking toward him. Trevor was certain there must have been a time longer than this when they'd both been working but hadn't said anything to each other, but he couldn't remember one. They were always going back and forth between the stores—okay, well, it was mostly Trevor going over to Snax 'N' More to annoy Kat, but still. That was what made this job bearable. Without her, everything that he did—standing here waiting for customers, smelling the congealing cheese on pizza, watching people wander by on their way to something more exciting—became oppressive. Unbearable. He was suddenly very aware that for most people, an airport was a pit stop, a dot on the map of their journey, but for him, it was his life.

It was the end of a journey. No, he wouldn't let it be that way. This was just a stop for him too, right?

Sighing, Trevor grabbed a rag to wipe down the counter. Again. Things wouldn't be so bad if people actually came by to order something and keep him busy, but it was after the normal dinner rush, and the airport was already empty enough as it was. As Trevor scrubbed the counter, he looked out of the slice of the window he could see at the gate located diagonally across from him. The Slice closed at eleven, but it didn't seem like he'd be able to leave anytime soon. He had been looking forward to being snowed in at the airport with Kat. Sure, it wasn't the most romantic of locations, but he could have made it work. Now, though . . .

"Hey!" A voice made him look up from the counters that really didn't need to be wiped down again. Trevor saw it was the kid, Adrian, who Kat had helped.

"Hey, man," Trevor said, setting aside the rag. "How's it going? How was the big date?"

Adrian smiled. "Good. She's in the bathroom. Thanks again for your help." He scuffed his sneakers on the tile floor.

"Sure thing." Trevor smiled, even though it felt like someone had punched him in the gut. "Glad it worked out for you." Adrian nodded, but didn't move. Trevor leaned forward, his elbows resting on the counter. "Need something?"

Adrian ran a hand through his hair. "I don't know. Maybe. You've dated before, right? Like, you know girls?"

Trevor gave a little laugh. "Uh, sure."

"I just . . . " The kid sighed. "I like her. But I don't know if she likes me. The only reason we did this whole date thing was so she could post pictures to try and get her ex to leave her alone. And sometimes I think she likes me, but even if she does . . . we're different. Like, sure, here at the airport we don't seem so different, but we come from different worlds. Literally—I'm moving out of the country in, like, a couple days." He fiddled with the hem of his shirt. "How do I know if she likes me? Or maybe it doesn't matter and it's a bad idea to try and date? What if she realizes she's too good for me, and dumps me? What if we can't make it work when we're so far apart, and one of us gets hurt?"

Adrian's eyes swam with confusion, and Trevor had to look away. "I don't know, man." He glanced at the store across the way. No sign of Kat. He shook his head, facing Adrian again. "I'm not really the best person to ask. I thought a girl liked me, and I liked her back, but now she's leaving, and I'm not sure of anything. Girls are hard. Dating is hard. That's all I can tell you."

Adrian's shoulders slumped. "Yeah. Okay. Thanks."

Trevor noticed a girl with red hair walking toward them, and Adrian turned to smile at her. He gave Trevor a nod before the two walked off together.

Trevor blew out a breath as he stood up straighter. Well, that was depressing. Did he really think that? That it was all too hard to do anything about? The old Trevor would have told Adrian to go for it, that if he liked this girl, he should do something big to wow her. But now Trevor had been shaken. Nothing seemed trustworthy in his world if his friendship with Kat wasn't solid. Who was he to give love advice?

Movement in the store. Trevor looked up. Kat was walking by the entrance, carrying a broom. Something in Trevor's chest tightened. He missed her. It had only been an hour, but he missed her. Kat disappeared from view, and Trevor wondered what he had done.

8:46 pm

Adrian's and June's footsteps were the only sound in the empty stretch of terminal, the echoing silence underscoring their lack of conversation even more.

They'd continued to hang out since their date, but things had shifted. Adrian knew June could tell, but he didn't know what to say to her. They had been sitting on that bench in front of the fish tank, and everything in him wanted to kiss her. Then after Mariel interrupted, it was like he could see himself as if he were watching a movie. There was June, who lived in Atlanta and had dated before and was only hanging out with him to get rid of her ex. And him, who was leaving the country soon and didn't know what his future would look like and had never had a girlfriend. It made his palms sweat thinking about it. She was only hanging out with him to pass the time, and once they left the airport, she wouldn't give him a second thought—just like the people from his school.

But he didn't know how to tell her that, so they'd wandered together, making small talk about Golden Hollow and movies and other books they read. It hurt to talk about something so shallow after knowing her story and her knowing his, but the idea of going deeper seemed dangerous. And yet, he couldn't *not* be around her, even though he knew that was the simplest solution.

Now their conversation had stumbled into silence, and Adrian was so busy worrying that June would make up an excuse to leave that he couldn't think of anything to fill in the quiet. When his phone buzzed, a wave of gratitude washed over him.

"Sorry," he said, grabbing his phone out of his pocket. He frowned. "It's Mariel. She says to come back to the gate ASAP and bring you with me." Adrian looked up at June, whose eyebrows were creased together.

"She said to bring me?" June asked.

Adrian nodded. "Yeah. Who knows what she has planned?" He cleared his throat. They had stopped walking and were standing underneath the buzzing fluorescent lights. "You don't have to come if you don't want to, though. I'll tell her you were busy or something."

"No." June shook her head. She offered him a smile. "I'll come."

June had the tiniest gap between her two front teeth, and every time she smiled at Adrian, it made his stomach feel like he had swallowed a dozen frogs.

"I mean," she continued, "it might be something good to post as a photo, you know."

Right. The frogs in his stomach turned to bricks. He simply nodded, and they turned around to head back toward the gate.

When they arrived, Mariel was waiting for them. "There you are!" she said. "Took you long enough."

"It's a big airport. Chill." Adrian rolled his eyes. "What's so important?"

Mariel grinned at them. "I have an idea."

Adrian and June exchanged a look. June had met Mariel for less than five minutes, but from her face, it seemed like even she knew this was a dangerous statement.

"What do you mean?" June ventured.

"C'mon, over here." Mariel led them farther away from the chairs where their parents and Sofia sat. "Okay, so you know our flight is canceled?" Mariel asked.

Adrian and June nodded. They had both gotten the text earlier. Adrian didn't need the text from his dad to know they would be spending the night in the airport. June had called her mom, who called the attached hotel, and then called her back to say there was no vacancy and her dad couldn't pick her up, so could she please stay at the airport till they figured something out? After hanging up, June had slumped down like gravity had doubled. Despite himself, Adrian had wrapped her in a hug, trying to ignore the little thrill in his chest when she leaned into him.

"Well, that means we'll be having Christmas morning in the airport," Mariel said. "Which sucks. But Sofia's first question was about Santa and if we can still

138

celebrate Christmas in the airport and if she'd get any gifts." Adrian's heart twisted. He hadn't even considered how Sofia might react. "So, I was thinking we could put together a Christmas party." Mariel beamed at them.

Adrian frowned. "Where?"

"Here, of course. In the airport." Mariel said this as if it were obvious, her arms spread wide to indicate the gate where they stood.

Adrian, however, was still frowning. "What kind of party happens at an airport?" He crossed his arms in front of his chest.

"One that's done out of necessity when your flight is canceled," Mariel snapped. "Think about it. We'll have it at midnight tonight, when it officially becomes Christmas. It'll be like combining New Year's Eve with Christmas, and we can invite everyone else stuck at the airport to cheer them up, too. Sofia would love it. You know how she loves meeting *everybody*."

"I don't know . . . " Adrian said, shifting his weight.

"I think it sounds like a blast!" June piped in. Mariel and Adrian turned to look at her. "I'm in. Plus," she added, with a glance at Adrian, "it'll be great for pictures."

"Yes!" Mariel cheered. They high-fived, then both turned to look at Adrian. Mariel raised her eyebrows, looking all too similar to the face she made when they were kids and she was about to call him a chicken. June's expression was more tentative, but still had a wide, expectant smile.

He should say no. He should go sit in his seat and play on his Nintendo Switch until he was tired enough to sleep. But instead, he said, "All right. I'll do it."

"Yay!" June cried, and threw her arms around him. Adrian caught her in the hug, and it was almost enough to make it all worth it.

June let go and faced Mariel, still standing close to him. "So. What's first?"

"Well . . . " Mariel said, a glint coming into her eyes. "We need to invite people."

"So, what, we just walk around telling everyone we see to come to Gate 14 at midnight?" Adrian asked. The thought of talking to random strangers made him itchy.

"We could . . . " Mariel's tone was heavy with mischief. "Or, I was thinking we could make an announcement."

"What?" June and Adrian said together.

Mariel nodded toward their left. They were located at the end of the terminal, where several gates lined a cluster of chairs with people from different flights scattered throughout. Most of the employees had left, but one middle-aged woman with tan skin and dark hair sat behind a desk in front of a gate, scrolling through her phone.

"There. They've got that microphone. I say we figure out a way to get on it and make an announcement to invite everyone all at once." Mariel's voice was hushed, as if the gate agent might overhear her from yards away, but still flush with excitement.

140

"Wait," June said. "Why don't we use an empty gate to make the announcement?"

Mariel shook her head. "I thought about it, but they turn off the mics when there's not an agent at the desk."

"Did you do *research*?" Adrian asked, eyebrows shooting up.

Mariel shrugged. "I wanted to see if my idea would work."

"What exactly *is* your idea?" June squinted at Mariel, as if trying to see her better.

The mischievous smile returned to Mariel's face. "You two distract the gate agent. Then I grab the mic, tell everyone about the party, and *voila*." She spread her hands apart again, as if she had completed a magic trick.

June turned to look at Adrian, her feelings clear in her eyes. *I'll do it if you will.*

So Adrian nodded. "Okay. I'm in."

"Me too," June said.

"Great!" Mariel clapped her hands together. "So here's the plan . . . "

Fifteen minutes later, Mariel had explained what each of them would do, and they'd taken their places. Since they were pretty sure Mariel and Adrian's parents wouldn't approve of what they were about to do, they'd also had to figure out how to handle them. They waited until Mom had taken Sofia to the bathroom, where they wouldn't hear the announcement, and Mariel had convinced Dad to take a walk through the airport with his headphones in. He had

141

recently discovered podcasts, and Mariel had been more than happy to download several episodes of his favorites.

Adrian and June were standing two gates away from where the agent sat, on the other side of a cluster of benches. His heart was pounding. Why was he so worried? Then he glanced sideways at June. Maybe the pounding didn't have anything to do with what he was about to do, and everything to do with who he was doing it with.

"Ready?" June looked at him, her eyes shining. She was loving this.

Adrian nodded yes. Then June dropped to the floor and started crying.

Even though he was expecting it, Adrian was still startled by the suddenness of it and how convincing it was. June had told them she did theater at her school, but he didn't think she'd be able to get *real* tears to stream down her face.

"My ankle!" she whimpered, clutching it. "Ow, ow, ow!"

"Honey, are you okay?" A woman passing by with a rolling suitcase stopped at the sight of June sitting on the ground, hands wrapped around her foot. "What happened?"

"I tripped," June moaned, rocking back and forth a bit on the ground. "I think I twisted it or something."

"Oh, sweetie." The woman clucked her tongue. "I've always said those sneakers like the ones you're wearing may be stylish, but they offer no support!" Adrian bit back

142

a laugh, and he could tell June was doing the same. "Are your parents around?" the woman asked.

June shook her head. "I'm flying on my own."

"Poor thing," the woman said, taking out her phone. "Here, there's a number to dial if you need medical assistance in the terminal—"

"No!" Adrian and June said at the same time. Adrian nearly shouted it, making the woman jump.

He cleared his throat. "Look, there's an agent right over there. I'll go grab her." Adrian jogged off before the woman could argue. A blond woman with a high bun also stopped to see what was happening. Mariel had counted on there being a bit of a scene that would make it seem more believable to the agent.

As Adrian raced to the desk, he saw Mariel sitting in a chair nearby, ostensibly distracted by her phone but clearly glancing up at the desk every few seconds. She shot Adrian a smile when they made eye contact. He rolled his eyes, but fought back a smile.

Adrian reached the desk, panting, and slammed his hands on the counter. The agent started at the noise. "I need help!" he said, trying to inject as much desperation into his voice as he could.

"What's wrong?" The agent, whose name tag said *Victoria*, asked. She reached for the phone at the desk. "Who should I call?"

"No, no," Adrian insisted, motioning for her to come with him. "It's over here. Follow me."

143

"I can't leave—" Victoria started to protest.

"This way. Please!" Adrian said as he turned and power-walked back to where he'd left June. He held his breath until he heard Victoria sigh, and then follow after him. He bit his lip to hide a smile. Mariel's plan might actually work.

Victoria caught up to him as he neared the benches and followed him to where June was still sitting on the tile floor. Her back was away from the gate so that when the agent faced her, she was looking away from the counter. June was still moaning, and several people had gathered around.

"What's wrong?" Victoria asked. The concern in her voice was almost enough to make Adrian feel guilty.

"My ankle . . . " June groaned. Tears still sparkled on her cheeks.

"All right, give her some space, everybody," Victoria said, shooing away the small group surrounding them.

As Victoria squatted down to be closer to June, Adrian glanced back at the desk. Mariel was behind it now, messing with the mic. He watched, waiting for the announcement to come, but Mariel was still fiddling with it. What was taking her so long? She looked up, and when she caught him staring at her, Mariel made an exaggerated *How do I do this?* gesture.

Adrian groaned, but June made a gasping noise at the same time, which covered it up. How did Mariel not know how to work the mic? Hadn't she done research or whatever?

"Okay, honey, let's get you up and to a chair, and I can use the phone at the desk to call a medic," Victoria said, wrapping an arm around June's shoulders to help her up.

"No, no," June insisted. "I—I don't think I can stand." As Victoria readjusted her position next to her, June shot Adrian a look that clearly said, *What is taking so long?*

Before Adrian could figure out a way to reply, the speakers overhead crackled to life.

"Attention, everyone in the airport right now!" Mariel's voice sounded distorted, but her excitement was obvious. "Please join us for a very special Christmas party at Gate 14 at midnight to celebrate, well, Christmas!"

"What the—?" Victoria looked up, realizing the announcement was definitely not a scheduled one. She spotted Mariel at the desk. "Hey!" Mariel gave a small wave, then sprinted away from the gate. "Hey, you!" Victoria shouted again, standing up.

"Time to go," Adrian muttered to June.

He bent down and helped her up as Victoria started to chase after Mariel. Then the agent stopped, apparently remembering the supposedly injured girl. When turned, though, and saw June standing and walking, her eyes widened as she connected the dots. "*HEY!*"

"C'mon!" June took off sprinting, and it was all Adrian could do to keep up.

They didn't hear Victoria's footsteps behind them, but still kept running until they reached a gate several numbers away.

"Oh my gosh!" June laughed, sagging into Adrian. "That was so much fun! I can't believe it worked!"

Adrian was laughing too, and as June leaned into him, he wrapped an arm around her without thinking about it. June wiped tears from her face—a combination of the ones she'd shed earlier and fresh ones from laughing.

"Do you think anybody listened? Will they pay any attention?" June asked, tilting her face up to look at him.

Adrian shrugged. "I guess we'll find out at midnight."

June smiled, still leaning on him. "I guess so." The gap in her teeth made Adrian catch his breath, and he fought to remember why this was a bad idea, but all the reasons he'd thought of earlier had flown out of his head. June's eyes had softened as she looked at him. He swallowed.

Then his phone buzzed.

Adrian stepped backward, and June stumbled as she caught herself. He tried to ignore the look she gave him as he checked his phone. "It's from Mariel. She says to meet her at Gate 24." He found the sign for the gate next to them—number 37. "We better get going."

"Okay," June murmured. She took a breath, like she might say something else, might ask something, but then she let it out, nodding her head back the way they'd come. "Lead on." Adrian did, trying not to wonder what June was thinking about.

8:50 pm

Keely stared at herself in the mirror, glaring at her reflection as if it were Wes staring back at her. How could he change his mind like this? And then assume that she felt the same way? She thought they were on the same page, but now she was starting to think they weren't even in the same book.

Taking a deep breath, she turned on the faucet. The water ran over her skin, and she tried to focus on the refreshing coolness. The air in the bathroom was pungent with the chemical smell of cleaning supplies, and she did her best to ignore it. But when Keely turned to the paper towel dispenser, she discovered it was empty.

"*Why* is *nothing* working today!" Keely yelled in the empty bathroom, slamming a hand against the plastic dispenser. "Ow," she muttered feebly, shaking her hand.

"Whoa!"

Keely whirled around at a voice behind her. Apparently the bathroom wasn't empty. Her face turned red as she gave a close-lipped smile to a Latina woman in her twenties who had just stepped out of a stall. "Sorry. I'm frustrated. I didn't think anyone was in here."

The woman chuckled as she walked to a sink. "You gave me a heart attack."

"Sorry," Keely repeated, tucking a piece of hair behind her ear.

"What are you mad about?" The woman made eye contact with her in the mirror as she scrubbed her hands.

Keely blew out a breath. "Nothing. My husband . . . nothing."

The woman laughed. "Ah. I see." She pulled a paper towel out of the dispenser on her side of the sink to dry her hands.

"Why are men so annoying sometimes?" Keely asked, starting to rub her face before realizing her hands were still damp. Frustrated, she swiped them on her jeans.

"That's why I gave up on them." The woman shot Keely a grin as she grabbed some paper towels from the dispenser near her. "Here," she said, handing them to Keely, who took them gratefully. "But dating women has its hard parts too, if that makes you feel any better."

Keely gave a small laugh. "Not sure it does." She tossed the used paper towels in the trash. "He assumed I changed my mind on a really big decision because he changed *his* mind, and now he's mad that I haven't actually changed."

The woman was quiet, looking into the mirror but clearly thinking of something else. Finally, she said, "I guess it's hard to see things from a different perspective, especially if you're not trying. You assume things are one way, and that everyone sees them the same, so it's hard to realize you might be wrong, or at least that you should explain what you're thinking."

She squeezed her eyes shut briefly, then opened them and turned to face Keely. "I ran into my ex-girlfriend here. Small world, right? I thought we'd been flirting all night, but she just freaked out and now I don't know what's going on. But maybe I've been doing the same thing as your husband and assuming she felt the same way I did, without actually asking her." She pulled a hair tie off her wrist and began scraping her dark hair into a ponytail, looking in the mirror again.

Keely sighed, some of the fight hissing out like she was a popped tire. "I don't know. Maybe I should try to see it from his perspective too. But . . . " She shook her head. "Even if I understand where he's coming from, I don't think I agree with him."

The woman let out a long breath. "That sucks. I guess you have to decide if it's a disagreement that you can get over, or if it's too big." She laughed, shrugging. "But what do I know? I'm just some random person you met in a bathroom who completely misread the situation with her ex all night."

Keely returned her smile. "I hope you work it out with her," she offered. "Or that you find someone way better and forget all about her. Either one works."

The woman laughed again, ducking her head down. "Maybe. I think . . . I'm pretty sure I want her though."

"Well then, what are you talking to me for?" Keely nodded toward the exit of the bathroom. "Go get her." The woman stood there for another moment, chewing on her lip. Keely's smile softened. "Is she worth it?" The woman took a breath, then nodded slowly. "Then go on."

"Okay." She smiled at Keely. "Okay. Thanks. I hope you figure things out with your husband. Whatever that ends up meaning."

Keely have her a half-hearted smile. "Me too." The woman turned and left the bathroom.

Keely looked at herself in the mirror. Could she see things from Wes's perspective? Or were they too far apart? She sighed, and walked out of the bathroom, her shoes echoing against the cold tile.

9:00 pm

Resa came out of the bathroom, electricity running through her veins. But as she looked around the terminal, the feeling started to fizzle. Why did Landry think they wouldn't work together? Was there something about Resa that Landry couldn't stand? But hadn't they spent the whole evening flirting?

She wandered through the terminal, adrift. Her flight was canceled. There was no way to drive in this storm. The hotel had no open rooms. Landry was nowhere to be found. How had a day that started out so well gone so badly so fast?

The snow outside was a white sheet against the window that stretched along what was supposed to be her departing gate. Resa plopped into a chair, figuring she had nowhere else to go. She felt too antsy to watch Netflix or be on her phone, though, so her gaze wandered around the terminal as she tapped her fingers on the narrow armrest. The airport had largely emptied out after the announcement that flights had been canceled—all the people smart enough to get rooms at the hotel early, she supposed. Then, out of the corner of her eye, she caught a flash of blond hair.

"Landry?" Resa sat up and twisted around to look at who had hurried by. No—a different woman with blond hair, walking briskly past her gate.

Sighing, she faced forward, and jumped, startled. Landry was standing in front of her. "What?" was all she could say.

Landry frowned at her, arms crossed in front of her chest. "Resa, that woman was like, fifty years old. Did you really think that was me?"

Resa snorted. "I only saw blond hair, okay? And I was desperate. You . . . disappeared." She tucked her hair behind her air.

"I know." Landry nodded, but didn't move to sit down, or even look all that apologetic. "I'm sorry about that."

Resa waited, expecting an explanation to come. But Landry stood there, fidgeting with the hem of her shirt, not saying anything. Resa didn't know what to say either—was there something she should apologize for? She didn't think so. Why had Landry come back, if she was going to stand here in silence? The low murmur of a cable news station on a TV in the gate filtered into the quiet. Resa grasped for something to say, but the whole situation was so awkward, her brain had packed up and left, leaving her with no words.

Then Landry's eyes cut to the right. Resa followed her gaze and saw a gray backpack that she recognized leaning against a seat a few chairs down.

Resa raised her eyebrows as her brain returned from its mini-vacation and started piecing things together. "You didn't come here for me. You were just getting your bag, and then you were, what, going to go hide somewhere and hope you never saw me again?" She tried to keep her voice even, but frustration and shock heated her tone.

"I . . . " Landry trailed off as she looked away. "I don't know what my plan was." Still, though, she bent down and retrieved her backpack, not making eye contact as she straightened and slung it over her shoulder.

"No." Resa stood up.

Now Landry met her gaze. "What?"

"*No*," Resa repeated. "You can't leave. Not yet." She took a deep breath, trying to recall how energized she had felt after her conversation with the other woman in the bathroom. It was like reaching for a fragment of a dream after waking up. "You spent this whole evening flirting with me, but then refused to consider the idea of getting back together. I want to know *why*." She pushed a few curls out of her face. "At first I thought, I don't know, you had just been passing time by flirting with me and didn't want it to be anything serious. Or maybe there wasn't actually anything between us, only two friends catching up, and I was totally misreading things. But I don't think it's either of those."

154

Resa fixed Landry with her stare, planting her feet. "I think you're scared. I think you have a chance at that happiness that we let go of when we were younger, and it scares you. I don't know why. But I do know that if you let go of it again, if we leave this airport without making up with each other, you're going to regret it way more than whatever happened in high school."

"Don't try to tell me how I feel," Landry snapped, her hands clenched into fists. "Just because you knew me ten years ago does *not* mean you know who I am now." Resa fell silent, her shoulders slumping. "We may have had fun back then, but we're different people now. Too different. Maybe you don't believe it yet, but you would, if we tried to date. I can't take that risk."

"Landry, I would never—" Resa stood, reaching out a hand to her.

Landry turned away from her. "I don't want to hear your promises and all the things you *think* you'd never do. Just let me go."

Resa yanked her hand back as if she'd been burned, then let it drop to her side as she watched Landry walk away.

9:12 pm

Trevor tapped out a rhythm on the counter with one hand. The other hand was scrolling through Instagram, but he wasn't taking in any of the photos. Even though he was looking down, Trevor remained acutely aware of the store across the walkway, waiting to see if Kat would appear again, debating if he should go over there.

The announcement system came to life with a voice, distracting him from his thoughts. He was usually able to tune them out, but this was different. It sounded like a young girl, and the words definitely weren't a standard announcement: "Attention, everyone in the airport right now! Please join us for a very special Christmas party at Gate 14 at midnight to celebrate, well, Christmas!" The speakers clicked off, and Trevor laughed to himself. The couple people walking through looked up at the speakers, as if that would reveal who was making the announcement. Did someone hack the system somehow?

Trevor glanced across to the Snax 'N' More. Everything in him ached to hear Kat's reaction to the announcement. He knew she would find it cute, and the party idea would intrigue her. Normally he would already be on his way to the store to spin wild ideas with Kat of the person who had made the announcement and whether or not they got caught. But now this pointless fight froze him.

Trevor thought back to their argument. He had been careless; he could see that now. It was Kat's dream, and he'd freaked out. But it was because he loved her, not because he didn't think she could do it or that he didn't believe in her. Surely if she knew that, she would understand his reaction. Right?

Sucking in a breath, Trevor locked his phone and looked at the store. Kat was nowhere to be seen, but the store didn't close until eleven, so she must still be in there. He glanced around. The airport was even emptier than earlier, which he hadn't thought was possible. Trevor chewed on his lip. The need to talk to Kat, to explain himself, to bring things back to normal felt like a drum beating in his head, louder and louder. His feet started walking before Trevor was aware of what he was doing, his footsteps matching the pounding of the drum.

Then he arrived at the front of the store and forced himself to stop. Was he really doing this? Yes. He needed to explain why he had reacted the way he had and convince Kat to forgive him. And maybe date him.

Looking into the store, Trevor didn't see her at first among the shelves of snacks and toiletries and overpriced headphones. Surely she wouldn't have left early? Even if she had, where would she go?

"Can I help you?"

Kat's voice startled him, coming from his right. Trevor spun and saw that Kat had been straightening a rack of magazines. Now she was staring at him, arms folded across her chest, waiting. His half-baked idea of starting with something casual about the rogue announcement went out the window when he heard her icy tone.

"Yeah, Kat, I, uh . . . " Trevor fumbled for words. He'd never had a problem talking to Kat, and so his inability to form a sentence made him even more nervous.

Kat didn't seem in any hurry to help him, though. She stared at him, one eyebrow raised as he stuttered. Finally, he managed to say, "We need to talk."

"*I* don't have anything else to say." She started to turn around.

"Wait! Please," Trevor said. She paused. "I'm sorry." Kat looked at him again, her face softer than before. "I know I freaked out. But it's because . . . well, because I love you, okay? As more than a friend." Kat didn't react, but Trevor rushed on, his heart thumping so loudly he wondered if she could hear it. "I was going to tell you how I felt, and then you got into this writing fellowship, and I freaked out. I don't want you to leave. I want to know what it would be like for us to date, for me to surprise you with flowers and go to dinner together and be the one you come to when you're sad. And if you leave, well, I wouldn't ever get to know that. And so that's why I was so upset when you said you were moving to New York. It's not because I don't believe in you or anything. I just . . . love you."

Trevor held his breath, a timid, hopeful smile on his face. Kat had barely moved the entire time he was talking. Now she took a moment to stare at him longer before speaking.

"That doesn't change anything," Kat said, her brow still furrowed. Trevor straightened, as if she had thrown something at him. "If you really loved me, you would have been *happy* for me. You're my oldest friend. You know how much I've dreamed of being an author and how big of a deal this is. But you only thought of how it would affect *you*. Do you see how selfish that is?" She shook her head, looking away from him. "I . . . . Thank you for telling me how you feel. I know that takes guts. But if you can't be happy for me when something huge like this happens, then I can't be with you. If you're going to use your feelings to try and guilt me into dating you or not go to New York or whatever your plan was, then forget about it."

Now Trevor gritted his teeth. "Seriously? That's what you think? Are you forgetting that you were pretty rude to me too?"

Kat threw up her arms. "What do you want? An apology? For telling the truth?"

"It's *not* true, and if you knew me, you'd know that of course I don't want to work at this airport forever!" Trevor was close to shouting now, but he couldn't help it. "The only reason I'm happy working here is because *you're* here. Of course I have dreams. But you never asked, did you? All you can talk about is your writing and your dreams and your big plans."

Kat's nostrils flared. "You never went to college because you didn't know what you wanted to study, which was fine, but then you settled into this life that was supposed to be temporary, so what was I supposed to think?"

Trevor rubbed his face with his hands. Christmas music still played through the store speakers, like a mocking soundtrack to their fight. "Would that be so bad? If this was my life? Being an assistant manager, on my way to a full manager? I make good money. I have a more flexible schedule now. What if I was *happy* with this? Would you not want to be with me because of it?"

"That's not fair." He could hear the anger heating up Kat's voice, and she lifted her chin. "You know I don't care what you do. You've always insisted that you have dreams, and I didn't think that meant this. But if you're happy, I wouldn't care what you did." She shook her head. "None of this matters. I don't want to be around toxic people who don't support my dreams."

Trevor turned to leave the store. "Well, neither do I. So I guess that's that."

"I guess so," Kat said as he exited.

Trevor stormed back behind the pizza counter, wishing that he could break something without having it come out of his paycheck. It felt like the only way to respond to the most important friendship in his life breaking down was to break something else. But it was all shiny tiles and stainless steel, reflecting back at him a million little versions of his loneliness.

9:32 pm

After their escape from the gate agent, Adrian and June met up with Mariel and followed her plan to prep for the party. They'd been put on food duty, so they wandered around to the different restaurants to see if they would donate any leftover food they had at the end of the day. They also invited the workers to the party if they were forced to spend the night at the airport. So far they'd had pretty good luck in both areas.

"Where to next?" June asked as they walked away from a Starbucks where the employee had promised to bring hot chocolate with her to the party.

"Um . . . " Adrian looked at his phone to refer to the text Mariel had sent with instructions. "Looks like we've covered all the restaurants on our list in the terminal. I'll text Mariel and see if there are any she hasn't gotten to yet." He tapped out the message, and then nodded to some chairs at an empty gate. "Want to sit down and wait?"

"Sure." June followed him to the chairs. The terminal felt almost peaceful now that the bustle of travelers

162

had died down and the view of the outside was nothing more than a white blur.

There were a few beats of silence, and then Adrian said, "So . . . can I ask what your ex did?" He'd been wondering all night, and now seemed as good a time as any to ask. "Unless you don't wanna talk about it." He leaned forward with his elbows pressing against his knees as he looked at her.

June blew out a breath that ruffled her bangs. "No, you probably deserve to know since you're helping me like this. It just . . . sucks." She scuffed a shoe on the ground, her fingers clutching the edge of the chair. "On the Friday after the semester ended, there was this big party. Kaden wanted me to go, but I was flying out for my dad's house early on Saturday morning, so my mom said no, and I kinda didn't want to go anyways, so that was that. But Kaden was pissed, and went anyway, which, whatever. I felt bad though—which, now I realize I shouldn't have, but he made me feel kinda bad—so I finally convinced my mom to let me go as long as I left by eleven."

Adrian had a sinking feeling in his stomach as June continued. "So I showed up at the house where the party is happening, and it's already nine thirty, but I wanted to show Kaden I wasn't a boring girlfriend. Or something like that. I don't know. But I'm wandering around the house, looking for him because he isn't answering my texts, and then . . . " She stumbled over her words, and when she continued, her voice was quieter. "And then I found him in the laundry room, making out with this girl on the soccer team. More than making out—his hand was—" She broke off. "Anyways. They stopped right after I came stumbling through the door, but I'd seen enough. I ran. Kaden followed me and was trying to get me to calm down, but I didn't want to hear it. I yelled at him—I don't even remember what I said—and drove back home. Then I flew out the next day and haven't seen him since." She sagged a little. "He's called and texted a few times, and I responded once that I needed space. So he quit, but I guess now that I'm headed back to Atlanta he thinks that's enough space." June didn't face him, instead turning to look at the window.

Adrian's blood boiled. What kind of jerk did that? Especially to someone as amazing as June. He wanted to say that to her, and more, to tell her how she deserved someone so much better than Kaden and that he wished he could be that person for her . . . but he stayed quiet. They were just friends. Eventually he said, "I'm sorry. That really sucks." He swallowed, before reaching out a hand to rest on her shoulder.

She turned back to him, tears lining her eyes. "It does." She ran a hand through her auburn hair, trying to compose herself. "Sometimes I wonder if I should hear him out. But what explanation could he possibly have? I don't want his promises that he'll be better. But I'm going to have to deal with it somehow, because I don't think he's going to give up before the next semester starts." Her lips curled into the barest of smiles. "Maybe our plan will work, and he'll back off."

Then her phone buzzed again. She looked down and grimaced. "What do you know? It's him." She chewed her lip, staring at her phone. Then she sighed. "I think . . . I'm gonna call him. Tell him it's over, for real." June stood up. "I'll be right back, okay?"

Adrian nodded and watched her as she walked away, around a corner away from the gate. He tapped his foot against the edge of the chair, the rhythm slowly increasing. One minute passed, then another. He wondered how it was going. He wondered how anybody could be as big of a jerk as Kaden. Sighing, though, he remembered people at his high school, at drama like this that had gone down. He knew there were cruel people in the world. He just didn't understand why it had happened to June.

Adrian checked his phone. Fifteen minutes had already passed. What had June meant when she said she'd "be right back"? Fifteen minutes seemed like a long time. What if he had said something terrible to her and she was crying somewhere? Or having to put up with some other crap from him? He couldn't stand it.

Pushing to his feet, he followed in the direction June had walked. He would just check, real fast, to make sure everything was okay. It was sort of on the way to the bathroom, so if everything was fine, he could pretend he had needed to get a drink or something.

Adrian rounded the corner. June was a few feet away, facing the window with her back to him. Since he couldn't see her face, he couldn't quite tell what was going on. She didn't seem to be crying, though. That was good.

He was about to turn around, satisfied she hadn't broken down because of the phone call, when she began talking, responding to something Kaden said. He couldn't help but overhear her.

"I know. I miss you." A pause as she listened, even as her words were a knife to his heart. She spoke again. "Can't wait to see you. I love you."

Adrian felt like the floor had dropped out from under him. He barely managed to stumble back to the chairs where he and June had been sitting. How could she say that to Kaden? To the guy who had broken her heart? She had been so dead set on not going back to him. He had even wondered if part of the reason was because she had feelings for *him*.

But he was wrong. She had never felt anything for him. She'd used him—maybe to make Kaden jealous, not to scare him off. The realization hit him like a ton of bricks. June had always wanted Kaden back, and now she had him. Why had he let himself feel anything for her? He knew how this would go. He never fit in anywhere, never clicked with anyone. Sure, he may have thought he had something special with June, but clearly she didn't feel the same. The only good thing was that Adrian had never told her how he felt, never given her the chance to reject him outright.

June reappeared, a tentative smile on her face as she rounded the corner and walked toward him. Almost sparkling. He wanted to throw up. She was truly happy, then, about getting back together with Kaden. He clenched his hands into fists. He wasn't going to let her reject him now. He'd done what she needed, and now they were through.

"Adrian—" she started as she got closer. But seeing the look on his face, she stopped short. "What's wrong?"

He swallowed. June didn't know that he'd overheard the phone call. Something about the way she held herself had shifted; she was confident, settled in herself. Because of talking with Kaden. Maybe she did love Kaden, did really want him back. Who was he to judge? What did she owe him, some random guy she'd met at the airport only a few hours ago?

June was still watching him, the happiness starting to slip off her face. No. If she was happy, he wanted her to stay that way, even if it wasn't with him. She deserved that much, even though it made everything in him ache.

He stood up. "I'm sorry. I should go." He couldn't look her in the eye.

She frowned. "What? What do you mean? Go *where?*"

Adrian grabbed his backpack and swung it up over his shoulder. "I'm sure you have some catching up to do, and I don't want to get in the way. Thanks for killing some time with me."

He turned, but June caught his arm. "What do you mean? Didn't . . . didn't tonight . . . " She stumbled over her words, but he cut her off.

"Tonight was fun. I liked hanging out with you. But now that you don't need me anymore, I'm gonna go spend Christmas Eve with my family. See if Mariel needs anymore help." June's hand dropped to her side. "Maybe I'll see you around."

The words tasted like ash on his tongue, but he turned and walked away. This was what she wanted, and it was all he could give her. She deserved better than Kaden, but if that made her happy, he wasn't going to stand in the way. But he also wasn't going to wait around for her to ditch him or listen to her talk about how happy she was to be back with Kaden. It was better for everyone if he left.

9:37 pm

"Another?"

Wes looked up at the bartender. Before tonight, he couldn't have told you that bars were open even on Christmas Eve in airports. He couldn't have described how the kitschy Christmas music playing over a speaker makes the place feel emptier than it is, which is saying something, because he's the only customer here. He wouldn't have known how a smile from the bartender laced with something between kindness and pity made him feel smaller instead of helping. Now, though, he knew all of that.

Wes shook his head. "No, thanks."

The bartender shrugged as he put away the bottle of whiskey. Then he turned back to Wes. "Stuck here for the night?"

He nodded. "Trying to fly to Seattle, but . . . " Wes gestured to the window outside, whited out with snow.

The bartender wiped down the counter. "Yeah. Haven't seen it this bad in a while."

169

Wes grunted, and the ice cubes in his glass clinked as he raised it to his lips and sloshed the dregs of the drink down. It was only his second glass, but he wasn't used to the altitude here, and his head was starting to feel fuzzy. Enough that when a woman who looked an awful lot like Keely appeared next to him, he started to wonder if he was hallucinating.

"What on earth are you doing?" she demanded.

Ah. So it wasn't a hallucination.

The barstool squeaked as Wes twisted on it to face her, setting down his glass. "Found this place after we fought. Been hanging out here since the flight is canceled anyways."

Keely ran a hand through her hair. Wes longed to do that, to feel her satiny hair slip through his fingers. Before he could reach out a hand, she spoke. "Come on. Can I talk to you?"

"Okay." Wes pressed his hands against the counter as he pushed himself up. He fumbled through his wallet to throw down cash for the bartender. "Thanks, man," he called. The guy waved at him.

"Glad you made a friend," Keely muttered as she steered him back into the bright lights of the terminal. Wes squinted at the sudden change from the dim bar interior.

He followed her as she marched out of the cluster of restaurants. When they reached an empty gate area, and Keely whirled on him. "Are you drunk?"

170

"What? No," Wes said, but Keely pursed her lips in a way that told him she didn't buy it.

"I can't believe this." Keely rubbed her face with her hands. "I wanted to talk to you and have an adult conversation, but you're drunk."

"I'm *not* drunk!" Wes said, although it was a little louder than he meant it to be. He made a conscious effort to lower his voice. "I only had two drinks, all right? I'm buzzed, at most. Still clear enough to talk to you, except you've made it clear you don't want to talk." He leaned against the pillar that was beside him.

Keely let out her breath in a hissing noise between her teeth. "I'm here now, aren't I? I want to try and see things from your perspective." It seemed sincere, but then she added in a lower voice, "Though this would have been better if I hadn't spent an hour wandering the airport looking for you."

"You could have called!" Wes protested this last statement.

Keely gave him a look. "Oh, really? I should have used a cell phone since it's the twenty-first century and not 1905? Why didn't I think of that?" She bonked her palm into her forehead in an exaggerated *Silly me!* motion. Wes swallowed. He didn't think this was going to go well for him. "Check your phone."

Wes dug through his pockets until he pulled out his cell. Four missed calls and several unread texts, all from

Keely. "Oh," he said, the word falling flat between them. "Sorry. I guess I didn't hear it."

"Clearly." Keely folded her arms in front of her chest. "But thanks for assuming it was my fault."

Wes forced himself not to roll his eyes. "Don't be like that."

"Like what?" Keely asked, now spreading her hands wide. "How else am I supposed to respond when you ask me if I did the most obvious thing? You always act like that, assuming the worst of me and acting like you know best."

Wes gritted his teeth. "Okay. This is obviously not about the phone calls."

Keely's arms dropped to her side. "Glad you figured that one out, Sherlock."

He decided to ignore that, instead pushing off the pillar to stand straighter. "Do you want to know why I thought you might have changed your mind about kids? Because I actually wasn't basing it on nothing, which you'd know if you asked."

Keely eyed him. "Fine. What made you think I would change my mind on such a huge topic even though we'd never talked about it?"

"When we babysat for Hailey and Nora's kids. A few months ago, remember?" Wes watched Keely's reaction carefully, trying to see if she had the same memories of that weekend as he did. Their friends had gone out of town for a short anniversary trip, and they'd agreed to watch their two boys for the weekend.

"After they picked them up, we both basically collapsed on the couch," Wes continued. He had replayed the moment so many times in his head, it was as vivid as if it had happened yesterday. "I said something about how fun it was, and it made me think that we could be parents. And you agreed, and said something about how you were so tired, but also it had been the most exciting weekend we'd had in a while. I thought . . . I thought that meant you were also thinking about what it would be like to have kids of our own." His eyes were still on her face.

Keely frowned, which was not a reaction Wes had hoped for. "Yeah, of course I remember that weekend. And I sort of remember you saying that after they left. But I thought you meant it, you know, theoretically. Like sure, we could handle being parents if we wanted to, but we didn't, so that was that. And . . . " She chewed her lip for a second, then continued. "When I said it was the most exciting weekend in a while . . . I was more talking about how we didn't do anything special with our weekends anymore. When we were first together, we always had something fun planned for the weekend, but that sort of stopped. I guess that was my way of trying to nudge us back into it. But I was thinking of going to the movies or something, not having kids."

Something inside Wes crumbled. He had been clinging to this memory for months now, convinced that Keely felt the same way he did. But she hadn't been thinking that at all. In fact, she was bored with their marriage.

"So you don't want to start a family," Wes said, his voice flat.

Keely's face had been hesitant, even concerned before, but now he saw anger harden her features. "I hate it when people say that. 'Start a family.' Are we not a family, the two of us? Is that not enough?" Her voice was louder now.

"I don't know!" Wes said, his volume matching hers.

Keely stepped back, as if he had slapped her. "You don't know if we're enough?" Her tone was quiet now, subdued.

"I don't—I didn't mean it like that," Wes said, taking a step toward her. "I just . . . I don't know what I want."

Keely's shoulders slumped. "Well. I guess I'll give you time to figure it out, then."

Before Wes could respond, Keely was walking away from him. Again.

9:49 pm

Charles twisted again in his seat, trying to find a comfortable position. These chairs weren't meant to be sat in for longer than a typical two-hour wait before a flight, that much was clear. He'd been alternating between walking around the terminal and sitting here, but even still his hip was starting to bother him. It was almost enough to make him wish he lived with Shonda and never needed to fly. Almost.

As if summoned by his thoughts, Charles's phone started to ring with a call from his daughter.

"You should be asleep," he answered. It was nearly midnight in Atlanta.

"Hello to you too." He could almost hear her rolling her eyes. "How's it going there?"

Charles looked around the airport. Everyone who could leave had already left, so he was growing used to the small group remaining. Even though he hadn't spoken to most of them, there was a sort of kinship formed by being stuck here together. "Things are actually going pretty well." Across the aisle from him, Sofia was asleep in Ellen's lap, and she looked close to drifting off herself. Jon was on his phone.

"Seriously?" Shonda said. "Aren't you sore?" She didn't need to say the words for Charles to know she was thinking, *This is why you should move closer.*

Charles sighed as he crossed one leg over the other. "I'll be fine. You don't need to worry about me."

"But I *do.* Because—" Shonda stopped short. Charles's eyebrows bunched together as he wondered what she wasn't saying. "Because you're my dad."

"No, honey, that's why *I* worry about *you.*" He kept his voice soft. "That's how it works."

Shonda blew out a breath. "If you'd left a few days ago, you would have already been here instead of snowed in at an airport."

"I know," Charles said, "but there's no point in dwelling on the past now." Mariel and Adrian entered the gate area, talking animatedly about something. Adrian dropped his backpack on a chair by his dad, and then the two were off again, presumably planning for the party they'd announced earlier.

He could hear the frustration in her voice. "Can't you at least explain why you waited?"

Charles hesitated. He knew he would need to tell her at some point. But it felt almost silly now, why he waited to fly out. Especially now that it meant he was snowed in. But he didn't regret it.

Shonda apparently interpreted his silence as a refusal. "You always do this. Act like you know best."

Charles frowned at her tone. "Sometimes, I do know what's best, for me."

"It's not just about you, though." He could nearly see her rubbing her forehead in frustration. "I'm worried about you, and I want to know you'll be safe. Mom would want that, too. You always think you're the only one who knows what's best. And look where it got you." She huffed out a laugh. "This is like when I went to college all over again."

Charles grunted. "English is not a useful major. You already know the language." He had worked for over forty years at a car manufacturing plant. Then his only daughter decided she wanted to do the most impractical thing at college.

"Dad, you *know* that's not what it is. And I've got a job now, so it worked out, didn't it?"

"You don't have a *job*. You've got dozens of little jobs lined up, and you never know when the next one is coming in." Sliding back into this argument was like when he would go on autopilot while driving home from work. The route was so ingrained in his brain he barely thought about it, and then he would suddenly look around and wonder how he got there.

"That's not true." Shonda's voice was heated. "I've got a steady income, and so does Jason. You know all this, but you insist on being stubborn. As usual."

Charles gritted his teeth, but didn't respond. This was why they had never talked much before Angie died. It always devolved into an argument about her college major choice or, as she got older, her career choice. He knew she was doing fine now, but why couldn't she see that it might not always be that way? If she had gone into something reliable—even teaching, like her husband—her life would be so much easier.

"Someday you'll understand that what you think is being stubborn is me just trying to give you good advice even though you won't listen." Charles gripped the phone more tightly.

"I can't deal with this right now." Her words were as sharp as the icicles forming on the eaves outside. "Maybe it isn't a good idea for you to move in with us. I don't know how much of this I could take."

She hung up as Charles winced. Why did every conversation they had have to end like that? Shonda had always been more motivated by her emotions than by logic.

He released a breath. Whenever he would say something like that to Angie, she had laughed at him. *Anger is an emotion, too,* she would tell him. *So is fear. And you're acting on both of them.*

He had always shrugged it off, but now, as he was trying to hold on to every memory of Angie, this one rattled around in his head.

As Charles gazed out the window, circling this advice from Angie around and around in his mind like it was a car he was inspecting, he wondered if she was right.

10:05 pm

Kat's chest was tight in a way that was uncomfortable and all too familiar. She tried to focus on the rack of magazines in front of her. Lining up the edges, noticing how the light glinted off the glossy covers. Sometimes she was able to ground herself in these small details, to distract her mind enough that it forgot about the anxiety that was a python winding around her rib cage.

But tonight it wasn't working. Her thoughts kept circling back to Trevor. His reaction to her news. His confession of feelings for her. How long had he liked her? More than that—he said he *loved* her. Did he mean that? Why would he say that and jeopardize their friendship? Things had been good the way they were. Why did he go and change them?

Kat chewed the inside of her cheek as she fiddled with a magazine cover. She was also changing things by applying and going to the writing fellowship. But she didn't want to stay here forever. Still, it was weird to think of living far apart from Trevor. She wasn't sure how she would have made it through high school and even college without him.

The idea of moving across the country from him made her hands clammy.

But that didn't mean she *loved* him. Right? And even if it did—which it didn't—he had messed things up by using his big declaration of love as an excuse for acting like a jerk. She meant what she'd said: If he really loved her, he'd be happy for her, and she didn't want to be with him if not.

Kat's hands shook, and it was a battle to get air into her lungs. She finally gave up on the magazines and went to stand behind the counter, squeezing her hands into fists. This was pointless. He wasn't worth it. There was nothing she could do about the blizzard. Logically, she should let it all go. But her mind was no longer responding to logic. With trembling fingers, Kat pulled out her phone to write, to try and escape into the world of her own creation.

It didn't help. Writing made her think about the fellowship, which made her think about Trevor. She bit her lip. If writing couldn't distract her, then what would work? Of course, normally when things got this bad, she would go talk to Trevor. He could always make her laugh, and he'd been friends with her long enough to know what *not* to say, which was difficult when talking with most people about her anxiety. He didn't judge her or tell her to "just think about something else."

Kat grabbed a box of travel-size hand sanitizers and started walking toward the shelf where they were kept, hoping the work would distract her. Her chest constricted again, but in a different way—in a yearning for things to be okay with Trevor, because she didn't want to lose him. He was her best friend. He sent her memes that he knew she would like and brought her pistachio ice cream when she was on her period and she didn't have to worry about him laughing at whatever was making her anxious and she could relax around him in a way she couldn't with anybody else—

The box crashed from Kat's hands to the ground. Did . . . did she like Trevor? Did she love him?

Before she could analyze that more, she realized the bottles were scattered around her, and one had popped open, leaving the sticky sanitizer in globs on the tile.

Kat groaned. "Seriously?" She turned to grab paper towels off the counter behind her. "Could tonight get any worse?"

As she bent to wipe up the hand sanitizer, a voice made her look up.

"Are you okay?" A girl, maybe high school age, rushed over to help. She had dark hair and tan skin.

"Yeah, I'm fine, just a klutz." Kat finished wiping the floor and started piling the bottles back into the box. The girl squatted down and picked up bottles too. "You don't have to help, it's fine."

"No worries, I'm happy to help." The girl smiled, and Kat returned it. They worked without speaking for a moment, the sound of bottles plunking against the cardboard box filling the silence, before the girl asked, "Having a rough night?"

Kat looked at her sharply. "What do you mean?"

"Sorry. I overheard you saying something when you dropped the box. About how tonight couldn't get worse." She shrugged, keeping her eyes on the last bottle as she put it into the box.

With the mess cleaned up, they both stood. Kat trudged to the counter and set the box down before turning to face the girl. She hesitated. "What's your name? I'm Kat."

The girl smiled. "Mariel."

Kat nodded, considering. Her chest was still tight. She didn't have Trevor to talk to. Maybe it was worth a shot to talk to this girl.

She sighed, turning to toss the used paper towels into the trash can behind the cash register. "Yeah. It's been kind of a crappy night, to be honest."

"I'm sorry," Mariel offered, leaning one hip against the counter.

"It's fine." Kat shrugged, tracing the edge of the cardboard box with her finger. "Guys are just annoying, you know?"

Mariel laughed. "Yeah, tell me about it. My ex . . . " She shook her head. "Want to talk about it? That's helpful sometimes, to me, at least."

Kat bit her lip. Was she really about to tell a stranger everything that had happened to her tonight? But maybe someone with a new perspective and zero skin in the game would be helpful. She launched into her story. "Basically, I got into this amazing program that meant I needed to move to New York. I was so excited, but my best friend freaked out and insisted I couldn't go." Kat smoothed out an imaginary wrinkle in her uniform shirt so she didn't have to look at Mariel.

"That sucks," Mariel said. "Like he didn't want you to leave, so he was a jerk about it?"

"Kinda, yeah." Kat sighed and looked up. "He came over and apologized, but it wasn't very good. But I also said some things that were hurtful, so I don't know." She ran a hand through her hair. "He said he only reacted that way because he liked me, but if he really liked me, wouldn't he be happy for me?"

"Yeah. I don't know." Mariel tapped her fingers on the counter. "Maybe . . . maybe he was scared. Not that it makes it okay, but at least there's more to it, you know? He wasn't just being a control freak."

"I guess." Kat chewed on her lip. "He's never done anything like that before."

"How long have you known him?"

"Since middle school."

Mariel nodded. "So if he's not usually like this, maybe you need to give him another chance. But only you can know that, right? Like I don't want to tell you to go back to some jerk who's always terrible to you or something," she added in a hurry, her eyes widening with concern.

Kat laughed, a little surprised at this insight. "No, he's really a great guy. It's why I was so surprised when he reacted this way." She fiddled with the flap of the cardboard box. "Which probably was also why I said some things I

184

shouldn't have." Her stomach got all twisty when she thought about what she'd said to Trevor.

Mariel nodded. "All I know is that I've been having a lot of change in my life recently, and it sorta makes me mad at everyone." She tucked a piece of hair behind her ear. "It doesn't make it okay, but I like to think it's not just me being a jerk."

"That's a good point." Kat folded her arms as she looked at Mariel. "What about your guy troubles? Is he worth it?"

Mariel paused for a moment, thinking. "Honestly? I don't know."

Kat raised an eyebrow. "Seems like an answer on its own, then."

Before Mariel could respond, a younger boy came around the corner. When she recognized him, Kat's face split into a smile. "Hey! Adrian, right? How'd the date go?"

Adrian's face, which had been relaxed and curious, darkened again. "Fine. Didn't work out though. I don't want to talk about it."

"Oh." Kat was tempted to ask what was wrong, but she knew when it wasn't the right time to pry. Instead she tilted her head and said, "Love sucks, right?"

Adrian looked at her for a second, but seemed to discern that it wasn't a patronizing statement, but a sincere offer of consolation. He gave her a small smile. "Yeah."

Kat nodded, satisfied. "What are you guys looking for? Anything I can help you find?"

"Well, we're planning a Christmas party—" Mariel started. Kat's eyes grew huge.

"Wait, were you the ones who made the announcement?" When Adrian and Mariel nodded, Kat clapped her hands together. "That was dope! I loved it! I'm definitely coming, by the way. And whatever you need from the store, let me know. I'll use my discount to help out."

Mariel grinned and launched into a list of items they needed to finish off the party. Kat nodded along, and after a minute, she realized her chest had loosened and breathing was easier. Still, something in her felt off. She tried not to think about it too much, but she knew that it had to do with Trevor.

10:18 pm

Landry wasn't sure how she ended up on the floor, surrounded by garbage. One second she'd been walking past a pizza place, trying not to think about how Resa had gotten her dinner from here and somehow made eating greasy pizza look cute. The next moment, a putrid smell had overwhelmed her before she felt a *thud* and then she was on the sticky tile floor of the airport.

"Are you okay?" A guy a few years younger than her, wearing the employee uniform of the pizza place, stood over her, staring down with something akin to panic in his eyes. "I'm sorry, I was taking out the trash, I didn't even see you!"

Landry pushed herself up, trying not to think about what she was lying in. "Um, yeah, I'm fine." She frowned. "What happened?"

The guy straightened and rubbed the back of his neck as Landry stood. "I think you must have been walking by right as I was taking out the trash—you know, it's a lot of bags, and I couldn't really see around them, so I assumed it was all clear when I came out, except . . . then I hit you."

"And the bag broke, it seems." Landry gazed around at the trash scattered across the floor.

"Basically, yeah." The guy surveyed the scene as well.

Landry snorted as she stood up. "Well, that would be my luck tonight. Getting body slammed by trash bags."

The guy let out a huff. "Rough night for you too?"

"You can say that again." She bent down to pick up a crumpled plastic container. "Got a new bag to fill up?"

The guy raised his eyebrows. "Oh, you really don't need to pick it up, I can do that—"

Landry shrugged. "I've got nothing better to do. Might as well help. I caused half the accident anyways."

"Oh-kay. Thanks. Let me grab one." He ducked around the counter and reappeared a moment later with a large black plastic bag.

"My name's Trevor." He squatted down next to her, and they began tossing pieces of garbage into the bag.

"Landry." They worked in silence for a minute, before she tilted her head to look at him. "So what made your night so bad?"

After a pause, he said, "Fighting with my best friend." Pieces of his curly dark hair fluttered as he let out a long breath.

"Ah." Landry tossed a plastic cup in the bag. "That sucks."

"What about you?" he asked, shuffling over to pick up some balled-up napkins.

188

"Getting snowed in at the airport on Christmas Eve isn't bad enough?" Landry started to sweep some escaped hairs back behind her ears, but decided she didn't want whatever was on her hands to get in her hair. She tried to blow them out of her face instead. The strands fluttered but didn't move. *Great.*

Trevor shrugged. "I mean, sure. But I figure if that's the only thing that happened, you'd be hunkered down at your gate, not wandering the terminal like a ghost that can't move on to the afterlife."

Landry was surprised at the laugh that escaped her. Trevor grinned. "Fine." She grabbed a plastic straw and threw it in the bag. "I ran into my ex at the airport, and thought maybe we could make it work this time. But . . . " Landry shook her head. "It's too difficult. We're just . . . too different."

Trevor nodded. "I'm sorry. That's rough."

Landry shrugged. "I should have seen it coming. She's great, but . . . " She trailed off, trying to remember all her reasons why it wouldn't work.

When she glanced up, Trevor was looking at her, waiting. She bit her lip as she tossed a crumpled paper towel into the bag. "I don't know. I should have known someone like her and someone like me wouldn't work." She swallowed, her throat tight. Maybe if they'd been together since high school, they could have grown into their lives together. But coming back like this after years apart . . . Resa

189

was smart and gorgeous and ambitious. And Landry was . . . Landry.

Trevor spoke, pulling her out of her thoughts. "Sometimes we like to ignore things we should know because we want something else to be true." His eyes flickered to a storefront over Landry's shoulder, and she got the feeling he was talking about something besides her situation.

Landry tossed the last piece of trash in the bag, and they both stood up, Trevor tying the bag closed.

"Do you have a sink in the back I could use to wash off?" Landry raised her hands up. There was no visible gunk on them, but they felt gross. She repressed a shudder.

"Oh, yeah, sure." He nodded back toward the storefront.

She followed Trevor behind the counter and into the kitchen. Grateful, she turned on hot water at the sink and began scrubbing her arms with soap. "So, what did you fight with your friend about?"

Trevor was leaning against the doorframe to the kitchen. He ducked his head down as he spoke. "She got into this writing fellowship that's in New York. Which I know is awesome, but I kind of freaked out. Because, um, I'm sort of in love with her? And so I don't want her to move. But when I told her that, it just made her more mad." He looked up at Landry, wincing a little. "So now I don't know what to do."

Landry turned off the water and shook her hands, before grabbing a wad of paper towels to dry off. "Yikes."

Trevor groaned. "I know. I messed things up. But I was trying to tell her how I felt! I had no idea she applied to this writing thing. I just got freaked out." He seemed to wilt against the side of the door.

"I know, but to her, you freaked out *at her* for doing something that, to be honest, sounds awesome and is probably a dream of hers, right?" Landry asked. Trevor nodded. "So that's a pretty selfish way to react. If you love her, you'd want to support her, right?" Trevor bit his lip.

Landry's gut twisted. "It just . . . really sucks to find out that someone you thought cared for you doesn't actually care about your dreams. To find out they're only focused on what they want." She trailed off, her throat tightening as if she might cry. She *would not* cry in front of this person she'd only met a few minutes ago.

Trevor studied her. "Is that what your ex did?"

Landry blinked. "Oh . . . no, actually. Resa was always really supportive. But my most recent ex . . . yeah, basically." She paused. "Yeah, Resa's been great about listening to what I want to do."

Trevor was frowning a little again as he stood up straighter against the doorframe. "So . . . is this about the ex you met tonight, or your other ex?"

Landry opened her mouth to respond, then closed it. "I . . . don't know." It was about Resa, right? Sure, Shelby had hurt her, but Resa had showed signs of doing the same thing—getting sucked into her career and realizing she was too good for Landry. Kind of.

Trevor shrugged. "Seems like an important thing to figure out."

Landry snorted. "Yeah. Thanks." She raised her eyebrows at him. "What about you? Are you gonna tell your friend you're sorry?"

He looked away from her, toward the dingy white tile squares on the walls. "I don't know. I mean, I am sorry. I know I messed up. But she also said some rude stuff to me."

Landry crossed her arms. "Listen, if you think being in love is all sunshine and rainbows, you might as well give up now." Trevor looked at her, eyebrows raised. "You're gonna fight. No matter who you're with. You're both probably going to say things sometimes that you regret. You have to figure out if it crosses a line for you and makes the relationship not worth it, or if it was something said in the heat of the moment that you can both apologize for later." She shrugged. "I can't help you figure that one out."

Trevor shoved his hands in his pants pockets. "Yeah. I guess that makes sense."

There was a beat of quiet. Finally, Trevor broke the silence. "Well, I should probably actually finish taking out this trash."

"Right." Landry nodded, and they headed back toward the front. "Sorry again about all that."

Trevor laughed. "I think it was mostly my fault. And besides"—he shot her a grin—"if it hadn't happened, I couldn't have given you all that great advice for your love life, right?"

Landry rolled her eyes, but she was smiling. "Sure, if you want to think of it like that." She raised a hand toward him as she walked away from the pizza place. "Good luck with your girl troubles!"

"Back at you!" he called, lifting up the trash bags.

Landry turned away to continue walking, but that piece in her that had felt so anxious and antsy before had seemed to calm down. Her feet were still walking through the terminal, but her thoughts were a million miles away.

10:32 pm

Even an hour after talking to Adrian, June still felt numb. After he walked away, June had sunk to the ground against the chilly window, wondering what had happened. She'd called Kaden and told him it was over, and even as he tried to make excuses, she stood firm. She didn't want to be treated like that, and it had only served to open her eyes to all the other problems in their relationship. When she hung up, she felt light enough to drift into the clouds. She even thought about telling Adrian that she liked *him* now, if she was brave enough. Then her mom had called to let her know she'd have to spend the night in the airport, apologizing profusely. She'd told her it was fine that she was still here, she loved her, she'd see her again soon.

Even that short phone call hadn't distracted her from what she knew: She liked Adrian. June couldn't put her finger on when it happened exactly, but at some point during the night, she realized she didn't want to leave the airport and never see him again. It wasn't just that they had similar interests. There was something about him, his quiet humor, his kindness, that made her feel comfortable

194

around him in a way she didn't with anybody else. After dating Kaden for months and feeling constantly like he wanted her to be someone different, hanging out with Adrian had given her the same relief she got when she finished a speech and debate tournament—the release of pressure, like she could breathe again.

But when she'd come around the corner, bursting to tell him that, he'd shut her down. Clearly he didn't feel the same way she did. He had been pretending all night. Just like she asked him to.

All June could think about was how she'd leaned on him and flirted with him and laughed with him all night, thinking there was something there, when really he'd been . . . what? Annoyed? Taking pity on her? Even embarrassed for her?

After June had dried her tears, she wandered closer to the gate where she was supposed to leave from, deciding to sit at the gate opposite her original one. Even though there was a chance of seeing Adrian here, she liked being closer to people. It was a little weird being in an empty airport, if she were being honest.

Settled in a chair, she took out an old *Golden Hollow* graphic novel to read. She wished she'd been able to finish the new one with Adrian, but that would obviously have to wait until she got to Atlanta. So June tried to lose herself in the issue she'd brought with her, but she had trouble focusing. Her mind kept wandering to Adrian, to her parents, to when her flight would be rescheduled, each

195

thought swirling around in her mind like the snow outside. She sighed, almost ready to give up on reading, when a voice interrupted her.

"*Golden Hollow*—my son loves those books."

June looked up and her eyes widened. Adrian's mom was standing in front of her, wearing faded jeans and a blue sweater. "Mrs. Addis!" she said before she could stop herself.

But it seemed like Mrs. Addis knew who she was, too. "June, right? No wonder you get along so well with Adrian, if you enjoy reading the same things." Her smile was kind, and June couldn't help but return it. "Do you mind if I sit?"

"Oh, no, go for it." June sat up a little straighter, instead of the exhausted slouch she'd been in before.

Mrs. Addis eased herself into a plastic chair across from June. "Do you know where Adrian is? We've only seen him from time to time since we got to the airport—since he met you, I think." She smiled again, but June bit her lip.

"I'm not sure. I haven't seen him in an hour or so." She meant to keep her voice neutral, but Mrs. Addis seemed to sense something anyways.

She paused before speaking, something shifting in her expression. "I'll call him, then, to find out." There was a moment of quiet, and Mrs. Addis appeared to be weighing her next words. "Has Adrian told you we're moving?"

June nodded, fidgeting with the cover of the graphic novel in her lap. She wasn't sure where the woman was going with this.

Mrs. Addis continued. "I figured. I hope that you and my son can still be friends, even once we leave. He had trouble making friends at school here and moving to Spain won't be easy on him. It looked to me like the two of you had something special together, and I think he would appreciate that, even if it's from far away." She tilted her head as she looked at June.

Her throat choked up as tears threatened to rise again. "I don't think he wants that." She knew there was no chance of keeping the betrayal and bitterness out of her voice this time. "I thought . . . I thought we were getting along well, too, but he didn't feel the same way. So, no, I don't think we'll be staying friends once we leave here."

Mrs. Addis studied her for a moment. June wished she would leave her alone. She knew she was seconds away from crying, but didn't want to do it in front of Adrian's mom.

But Mrs. Addis didn't move, and eventually she spoke. "I'm sorry to hear that. Adrian's had a rough time once he learned we were moving. As I said, he didn't have a lot of friends from school, but those he did have. . . . He drifted away from them just before we left. Stopped hanging out with them, stopped playing video games over the internet with them. I don't really get that part, but it seemed like a big deal." Mrs. Addis let out a long, weary breath as her gaze turned distant, like she was no longer actually looking at June. "I'm probably overstepping here, and I barely know you, but I think Adrian does like you, based on what I've seen and heard. If I had to guess, I would say he's scared. It's what made him lose touch with his friends, too. He'd rather be the one pushing people away than getting pushed." Mrs. Addis rose from her chair. "If he hurt you too much to forgive him . . . well, I'd understand. But if you still feel anything, I think Adrian could use someone willing to fight for him." She glanced out the large window to her left. "I should get back to my daughter. I hope you weather the storm well."

"Bye," June said as Mrs. Addis turned and walked back to the gate. Was she right? Had Adrian broken things off with her because he was scared? She chewed her lip. If so, would he change his mind? Was it even up to her to change it? Shouldn't he be brave enough to come around?

She stared out the window at the blizzard whirling outside, thinking about Mrs. Addis's words, and how she was pretty sure she wasn't talking about the snowstorm.

10:44 pm

Wes stood in front of the vending machine, studying his options. It seemed like it had been days, not hours, since he'd eaten that Panda Express for dinner. All the stores he'd passed by were closing, so when he happened across this vending machine, it looked like his best option. He finally decided a package of peanut butter crackers sounded good. It was one of those new machines that had a card reader, so Wes pulled out his card and slid it in. The machine beeped at him and spat it back out.

"Come on," Wes muttered, trying again. Same thing. "You've gotta be kidding me." He whacked the card reader a few times and only succeeded in making his hand sore.

Wes grimaced as he shook out his hand, wishing . . . he didn't know what. That the vending machine would work. That their flight wasn't canceled. That he and Keely hadn't fought last night. That they both wanted kids. There were so many things he wished.

Finding out Keely still didn't want kids was like a kick to the gut. How had he read that situation so wrong?

Or had she actually thought about having kids that weekend, but now didn't want them and wouldn't tell him she'd even come close to considering? He knew they had talked about it when they were dating, but he was so young then. Barely thirty. How was he supposed to know that he might change his mind later? And was it so unreasonable to think that Keely might too?

A sudden clattering noise startled Wes, making him spin around from facing the useless vending machine. A man in his forties bent down to the ground, picking up several empty water bottles rolling across the tile floor. When the man looked up, Wes realized he was the dad of the family that was in the gate with them, and who he had stood behind in line for Panda Express.

"Here, man, let me help." Wes walked over and crouched down to pick up two of the bottles.

"Thanks," the man said with a laugh as he grabbed the other two. "I was sent on a water bottle refill run, but I might have bitten off more than I could chew."

Wes smiled. "Want help with filling them?" They stood up.

Relief washed over the man's face. "Do you mind? If you'll hold them while I fill up one, that would be great."

"Sure." Wes figured he didn't have anything better to do with his time.

As they walked to the water fountain a few yards away, the man introduced himself. "I'm Jon."

"Wes." He paused. "You're flying with your family, right? Couple kids?"

Jon nodded. "Yep, that's us." He had a deep, throaty laugh. "I'm sure my kids are loud enough that everybody left in the airport can recognize us by now."

Wes grinned as they reached the water fountain. "They seem pretty well-behaved." He took three of the water bottles from Jon, who busied himself with filling up the final one he held, a red bottle decorated with race cars that clearly belonged to a child.

Jon chuckled. "I'm glad they've got you fooled." He glanced up from the water fountain. "And you're traveling with your—wife, girlfriend?" He grimaced. "Or maybe sister and I just made it weird."

Despite himself, Wes laughed. "You had it the first time—wife. Going to her parents' for Christmas. If we ever make it out of this airport."

Jon finished filling the first water bottle, capped it, and handed it to Wes, then took an empty blue bottle from the crook of Wes's left arm. "Yeah. We're trying to make the best of it, but it's been a rough night for everyone, far as I can tell."

Wes was quiet for a moment. He had no idea what this man was going through. Maybe his fight with Keely was petty in comparison to what other people at the airport were experiencing, even if it still hurt him.

Jon looked at him as he swapped the full blue water bottle for an empty silver metal one. "I'm getting the sense that it's been a tough time for you, too."

Wes chewed on the inside of his lip. "Yeah . . . my wife, Keely, and I . . . we got into a fight last night, and it exploded earlier this evening. So being stuck at an airport has not helped anything."

Jon winced. "Yikes. That doesn't sound fun."

"Yeah. You can say that again." Wes paused, wondering if he could ask Jon for advice. He was older, seemed to be happily married, with three kids. This could be exactly what he needed. Keely was always talking about how the universe had a plan. Maybe she was right. "Can I ask you something?"

Jon turned to him, finished filling the third water bottle. "Go for it. Can't guarantee I'll answer, but you can ask." He smiled at Wes as he retrieved the final water bottle, a heavy glass one with a floral pattern.

"Well . . . this fight we're having . . . basically, I want kids, and she doesn't." He saw Jon's eyebrows pop up, but the man didn't say anything. "It feels like we're at a standstill, and she won't consider anything else. I don't know what happens next."

Jon didn't say anything while he finished filling the water bottle. As he screwed the lid on, he turned toward Wes. "Well, first, is this the first time you two have talked about having kids or not?"

Wes shook his head. "Before we got married, we both agreed we didn't want kids. Then a few months ago, I made a comment about wanting to be parents, and I thought she agreed. But when I brought it up today . . . . Yeah, I misunderstood."

Jon nodded slowly, as he crossed his arms in front of him, still holding the water bottle. "So you've realized you want something else."

Wes adjusted the three water bottles he was carrying, not wanting to look at Jon. "I guess. Yeah. I mean, I know I said one thing, but is it my fault if I've changed as I've gotten older?"

Jon shook his head. "It's not. But you can't expect her to change in the same way." He tilted his head. "If there's one thing I've learned in marriage, it's that you can't get mad at someone for being who they've always been, instead of who you *think* they should be." Wes didn't have an answer for that.

"There have been plenty of times I get frustrated with my wife or my kids or my in-laws, but they're just being who they are. Who they've always been. Once I accept that, my life gets easier, and usually we can find a compromise." Jon looked at Wes, who finally met his gaze. "So, I don't think you can get mad at your wife for being who you knew she was when you got married. But maybe there's room for compromise, or change. Or maybe the two of you have grown too far apart." Jon shrugged. "I'm not the one who can decide that."

Wes nodded. "Yeah . . . thanks."

"Sure thing." Jon cradled the water bottle in one elbow and held out his other arm. "I think I can carry the rest of them back, if you'll hand them to me." Wes did so, one by one. "Thanks for the help." Jon began walking off.

"Sure. And thank you!" Wes called after him.

"Good luck!" Jon said over his shoulder. "And merry Christmas!"

Wes wandered back toward the vending machine, but didn't bother putting his card in. He found that his appetite had disappeared. Instead, he took a deep breath and headed back to their gate.

10:57 pm

"Charles, how're you doing?" Ellen's question broke into his thoughts. She had been asleep in her chair for the past hour or so and woken up a few minutes earlier.

Charles turned from looking out the window to smile at her. "I'm holding up all right, thanks for asking. Not sure what sort of welcome I'll be headed to when I get to Atlanta, though." He said this last part with a smile, but Ellen frowned.

"What do you mean? Is your daughter okay?" Concern creased her forehead.

"Yes, she's well. Everything's fine. She's upset with me though. Both because I won't move in with her family, and because I waited so long to fly out." Charles sighed and shifted his weight in the chair. "We've never seen eye to eye, and I was hoping it would get better after Angie passed, but it's still hard."

Ellen smiled, her eyes filled with kindness and understanding. "It might get better with time. You're both going through a lot still, dealing with all the grief that comes with a death of a loved one. It takes time to adjust."

Charles glanced away, his throat tightening. "I supposed you're right."

Ellen rested her elbow on the arm of the chair and leaned her head on her hand. "If you don't mind me asking, why did you wait so long to fly? It's something I've been wondering about all the other people at the airport right now, but you're the only one I can probably ask." She readjusted how she was sitting, careful not to wake Sofia, who was asleep with her head in her mother's lap, curled up with a tattered giraffe stuffed animal.

"It's a good question. I've wondered it too, about everyone else flying out today." Charles looked around the airport.

"You don't need to answer if you don't want to," Ellen began, but Charles shook his head, waving off her concern.

"No, no, it's all right." He rubbed his head. "I'm a little embarrassed, is all. It seems silly to tell someone else." Charles took a breath. "But I'll have to tell Shonda at some point, too, I'm sure, so I might as well practice on you, as it were." He smiled, and Ellen returned it.

After taking a breath, he started speaking. "Every year at Christmas, my wife and I had a tradition. We would read that old short story, 'The Gift of the Magi.' Do you know it?" Ellen shook her head no. "It's a classic. Remind me later, and I'll get one of your kids to look it up for you." He shot her a grin. "It's about a married couple trying to find Christmas gifts for each other even though they're desperately poor, and in the end they come to realize that their love is enough."

Charles's gaze drifted out the window. "Angie and I started reading it to each other when we were first married. Nearly as poor as the couple in the story. We kept doing it every year on Christmas Eve, just the two of us. Even when we had Shonda, we'd read it to each other while wrapping gifts late at night after she was in bed. A quiet moment during a busy season that we could share together."

He paused, remembering all those nights over the years, snow drifting down lazily out the window, as they read the short story to each other. His lips fluttered into a smile. "Anyways, I realized this year . . . well, I didn't want to let the tradition stop. So I decided to go to her grave and read it out loud to her." He shook his head. "Even as I say it now, it sounds foolish, but it felt right. So I didn't want to fly out before Christmas Eve so I could read it with her today, like we always do." Charles cleared his throat, working out the lump of emotion that had lodged itself there.

Ellen was quiet, letting him remember the morning. The snow had only started coming down a few hours before, not in the angry, aggressive way it was now, but falling lightly, like in years past. He had stood by her grave, wrapped in the strange sort of quiet that always came with new snow, his hands gripping the few printed-out pages with the story on it. His voice had only quivered a little as he started reading it to her, but by the end he was almost too choked up with tears to finish.

Charles shook his head a little bit, surfacing from the memory. "Anyways, there it is. An old man being sentimental, and now I've gone and gotten myself snowed in at the airport."

Ellen tilted her head at him. "I think that's a beautiful tradition, Charles. And I think it's good you kept it, even if it means you might spend Christmas morning here. I'm sure your daughter would understand if you told her."

Charles remembered when he had spoken with Ellen's daughter, Mariel, and made her promise to be honest with her parents about how she was feeling. Maybe he needed to take something of his own advice.

He nodded. "Thank you for listening. You're kind to let me go on about it." He adjusted his coat, which he had laid over his lap, the closest thing he had to a blanket. "How are you handling things?"

Ellen stroked Sofia's hair. The girl shifted and sighed in her sleep a little. Ellen's mouth creased into a smile. "I'm doing okay. I'm grateful for my family, and this opportunity for Jon, and I really am excited about moving to Spain. A new adventure. But it's hard. I didn't want to throw off our kids' lives like this, and the decision to travel around Christmas. . . . " She sighed, her hand still on Sofia's head. "It probably wasn't the smartest, but the tickets were cheap, and who could have expected a snowstorm?" Ellen

208

looked up from Sofia. "I worry for the kids, how it will affect them. I think, ultimately, it will be a good experience, something they're grateful for. But maybe I'm wrong. I know in the short term it will be hard. I don't want them to be angry at us, and I want them to give Spain the chance to be a home." She pressed her lips together in a thin line.

Charles made an understanding noise. "I'm sorry. I know that as a parent it's difficult to hope that your kids will trust you know what's right."

Ellen nodded, her eyes softening as she studied Sofia's sleeping figure. "Right now, I'm taking it one step at a time. First, this snow needs to stop so we can fly out of here."

"Amen to that." He smiled.

"Here we go!" Jon grinned broadly at them as he walked up, holding an armful of filled water bottles. "For you." He handed a bottle back to Charles, who accepted it gratefully. He gave another to Ellen, set one on the floor in front of Sofia, and took a big drink out of the final one.

Charles was glad to see Jon back and thankful for the conversation with Ellen. It seemed like a weight had been lifted off his chest, and he couldn't help but feel that if he had to be snowed in at an airport, he was glad it was with them sitting nearby.

11:16 pm

Resa closed her eyes and breathed deeply, listening to the gentle instructions given by the woman leading the yoga routine on YouTube. She had sought out a quiet corner in the second level of the airport to do some yoga in an attempt to get her mind off Landry. As her legs and arms moved through the stances, though, her thoughts still drifted toward Landry, no matter how hard she resisted. What did she mean when she said that they were too different? That she would realize that if they tried to date? Did it have something to do with her most recent ex?

As Resa moved into tree pose, bringing her hands together in a prayer-like position at her chest and one leg bending up until her foot rested against the knee of her other leg, she gritted her teeth—which was typically a sign that yoga wasn't working, but she ignored that for now. Steady breaths to focus on not wobbling.

"Um, should I come back?"

Resa's eyes sprang open, and any steadiness in her body disintegrated. She let out a yelp as she toppled to one side, even as her mind whirred. Was that Landry's voice? Or was she so obsessed that she was imagining it? That would be embarrassing and awful.

But it became clear she hadn't imagined it, as her fall was stopped midair. When Resa looked up, Landry was grinning at her, laughter sparkling in her eyes.

"Hey," Landry said, biting her lips to keep back a smile that peeked through anyway.

Resa's cheeks heated. "Hey."

"Didn't mean to scare you." Landry helped stand her up straight but didn't step away once Resa was on her own two feet. Jitters danced in her stomach.

"I was trying to clear my mind." Resa left it at that, but what she wanted to do was demand that Landry explain *right now* why she had reappeared.

Landry nodded, as if she knew exactly what Resa had been trying to clear her mind of. "Can we sit down?"

They settled into the row of seats nearby. Most of the light on this level came in through the skylights, which meant that at this time of night, the area was dim and shadowy. It made Resa feel like they were the only two people in the world right now.

After they sat down, Resa waited, trying not to fidget. She wasn't sure about much, but she felt certain that Landry should be the one to start this conversation.

After a moment, she did. "So, I've been doing some thinking. Since I . . . yelled at you." Landry's voice sounded very small, smaller than Resa had ever heard it. It made her want to reach out and squeeze Landry's hand, but she forced herself to listen to her words and keep her hands in her lap. "Which, first off, I'm sorry about. I think when you said I was scared, well, you were kinda right, and that made me angry. But I want to explain why I was scared, because it's not exactly the reason you thought it was."

She took a deep breath, then released it, making wisps of her hair flutter. "My ex, Shelby—she basically dumped me because I wasn't good enough for her. She thought the bakery was a waste of time, and that if she was going to climb in her career, she wanted someone equally ambitious."

Rage ripped through Resa at this person who had hurt Landry, who was so ignorant she couldn't see how much work Landry had put into her dreams. She clenched her hands into fists, letting Landry talk before she demanded the full name and address of Shelby to go egg her house.

"I was supposed to spend Christmas with her family, so the breakup caught me totally off guard. And yeah, it kind of wrecked me." Landry twisted her hands together, not meeting Resa's eye. "So when I ran into you and you mentioned your job kept you so busy, I thought you'd be the same as Shelby. I didn't want to risk getting hurt again. I still don't."

Something inside Resa crashed and collapsed. This was her worst fear of where this speech had been leading. To Landry saying no. To knowing that she would live in the same city as Landry, but never see her. She looked away as her eyes filled with tears.

But a soft pressure on her hand made her glance down. Her chest expanded as she realized it was Landry's hand on hers, squeezing gently. Resa dared to look up at Landry, who wore a soft smile.

"But I was wrong, Resa," she said, barely above a whisper. "That was fear talking, but I'm tired of being afraid. I want you. I told myself you were no different than Shelby, but I know that's not true. You're smart and ambitious, but you're also kind and caring in a way that she never was." With her other hand, Landry brushed a curl out of Resa's face.

Everything in Resa yearned to close the distance between her and Landry's lips, but she made herself speak. There was something she needed to say first.

"I'm so sorry you had to go through that." She turned her hand over so she could lace her fingers through Landry's. "I meant it earlier when I said it was her loss. You're amazing, and anybody who doesn't realize that doesn't deserve you. Even just from social media, I can see how much work you put into your bakery and going after your dreams."

Landry smiled. Resa did too, but kept going. "Also, you should know that the reason I applied to this new job is because I *don't* want work to consume my life. I love my job at Mercer, but there are some messed-up work dynamics that mean I'm basically always on call. I thought I loved the busyness, but I realized it's not worth it if I can't actually have a life. I'm hoping this new position will let me do that." She took a deep breath. "I can't promise that I won't get called in on the weekends sometimes or get lost in my work. But I promise that I'll never get bored of you, never put you second. I did that back in high school when I was too scared to try long distance, and I've regretted it ever since. I won't be perfect, but I'll keep trying."

Landry tucked another of Resa's curls back, and then let her hand linger on Resa's cheek. "Perfect is boring. I'd rather be with you, and all your mistakes and all my mistakes, than with anybody else." And then Landry leaned forward and kissed her.

Kissing Landry was both like being transported to the past but also freezing time itself. It had the same heady, overdrive energy that it did in high school, the thrill of a first kiss, but also it was so singular, so of this moment, that Resa couldn't have imagined anything like this ten years ago. Landry slid her hands into Resa's hair until her fingers were tangled in her curls, and Resa wrapped her arms around Landry's neck. It was exciting and new but also felt like returning home.

After a time that could have been mere minutes or long hours, they broke apart, giggling and breathless like they really were back in high school.

Resa bit her lip, smiling at Landry. "What now?"

Landry grinned back. "Well, I heard there's this killer Christmas party that's supposed to happen at midnight. . . . " Resa laughed, and it made Landry's smile grow. "Wanna go with me?"

Resa raised an eyebrow, bumping her shoulder into Landry's. "What, like a date?"

Landry shook her head, and Resa frowned. "No," Landry said, taking her hand. "Like as my girlfriend."

As an answer, Resa simply leaned in, lightning pulsing through her veins, to kiss her again.

11:28 pm

Kat wandered around the airport, searching for Trevor. When she had closed Snax 'N' More at eleven, he had already left The Slice. Surely he didn't go home—no one was leaving, not with the snow still piling up outside. But he wasn't answering her calls, and he wasn't in any of the normal places they sometimes hung out on breaks during their shifts. So she decided to walk, figuring her legs could use the stretch and she might run into him along the way.

She wanted to be back in time for Mariel's midnight Christmas celebration, but that gave her half an hour still. Kat tried to plan out the words she wanted to say to Trevor in her head, but she was better at writing than speaking, and her thoughts kept getting jumbled. She wished it wouldn't be rude to text him an apology, not because she was afraid to say it in person—although she was—but because everything in her mind always made more sense once she had a chance to write it out. Maybe she could write out her apology and practice it like a monologue before she saw him?

Too late. There he was, coming out of the restroom a few yards ahead of her.

"Trevor!" she called. He turned, and his eyes grew huge. Did he look a little disappointed?

"What are you doing here?" he asked as she came closer.

Kat stopped short. "Looking for you, obviously. Why are you all the way down here?"

"I was doing something," he said, shoving his hands into his pockets. "Why do you care?"

She ran a hand through her hair. "Okay, will you just listen for a second? I have something to say to you." Trevor opened his mouth like he might argue, but she plowed ahead. "So I've been thinking about what you said, and I'm sorry. I don't care what you do with your life—I mean, I *care*, but, like, in the sense that I want what's best for you, and whatever *you* want for you. So if you want to keep working here and moving up the ranks, that's awesome, and I'll totally support you. But if you want to go to college or go get a different job, I'll also be there. Basically, I know you're not some lazy slob, okay? I know you've got a lot of big dreams."

Kat took a deep breath and stood a little straighter. "I won't lie and say that it's okay that you reacted the way you did to my news about the writing fellowship. It hurt, and I don't think it was a good moment for you. But I also think I know you pretty well, and you didn't mean it. I hope you didn't, anyways. I'd like to forgive you." Kat had been looking anywhere but at Trevor, but now she met his gaze.

He stared at her for a second, and for the first time since they'd met, she couldn't read what he was thinking. Then he let his breath out in a huff. "C'mere." Trevor spun on his heel and walked away.

Kat blinked. "What?"

"Follow me!" he called back over his shoulder.

Frowning, Kat did as he said, walking past the bathroom and closed-down shops where they'd been standing. They were now in the darker part of the terminal, with most of the lights shut off for the night, where she'd suggested Adrian take June for their date.

A couple gates in, Trevor stopped walking and turned to face her. "Okay, I'm a little mad at you."

Kat frowned. That was his reaction to her apology? "What?"

"I was gonna do this big-gesture thing, but then you came and *found* me, so it's not even set up and I didn't have time to practice, but . . . here."

He bent down and took hold of something near the wall that Kat couldn't make out in the dim light, until he plugged the end of it into an outlet. The space burst into light, the strands of twinkling bulbs illuminating a large banner stretching between two pillars that read *Welcome to New York!* Beyond it, long paper rectangles were taped to the window, with small squares cut out to look like windows—it was the New York City skyline, Kat realized.

218

She turned in a daze to Trevor. "What is this?"

Trevor had been hanging back by the column where he'd plugged in the strand of lights, hands stuffed in his pants pockets, but now he stepped closer to her. "It's my big gesture. I was gonna have a song playing, but I didn't have time to pull it up, so, you know, imagine it in the background." He swallowed. "I'm sorry I was a jerk about you getting the fellowship. It's amazing, Kat. It really is. And so are you." Kat blushed. Trevor held her gaze, though, and she found that she couldn't look away. "I should have reacted that way from the start. You're right. I was being selfish when you first told me. I messed up. But like you said, I hope that was just one bad moment out of all the time we've known each other, and that you can forgive me."

Kat nodded, smiling. "Definitely." She looked around at the decorations. "Where did you even get all this stuff?"

He shrugged, not taking his eyes off her. "Your buddy Adrian left the lights here from his date. The buildings are strips of parchment paper from the kitchen that I cut holes into."

Kat laughed. "I'm impressed." She turned to face him again, tucking her hair behind her ear. "You know, before you freaked out, I was gonna ask you if you wanted to move to New York with me. We could get one of those tiny apartments that's the size of a broom closet together and live like starving artists."

Trevor blinked. "Wait. Really?"

"Yeah, you dummy." She shoved his shoulder playfully. "I didn't want to leave you any more than you wanted me to leave."

Trevor grinned, a mischievous glint in his eye. "Is that so?"

"Yeah." Kat smiled, but inside her stomach was fluttering. "You've been my best friend for ten years. I can't imagine life without you popping in constantly to annoy me."

He stepped closer to her, and though she knew they'd stood this close before, it felt different now. Heated. "Really? That's the only reason?"

Her mouth was dry, but she managed to say, "What else would there be?"

Trevor's gaze flickered from her eyes to her lips. "I was hoping it had something to do with my charm, my sense of humor, my chiseled face. . . . "

"You're stubborn, you know that?" It came out breathless, though losing its push since she was, in fact, distracted by his face.

"Right, my stubbornness too." His lips pulled into the softest of smiles. "Any other reason you'd want me to come to New York with you?"

Kat's stomach did a flip-flop as she said, "And because I love you, you idiot."

Almost before she had finished the sentence, Trevor was bending down and his mouth met hers. She wrapped her arms around him, letting the warmth of him flow into

220

her. She'd kissed her share of guys and girls before, but this was different. This felt right, like she'd been waiting for it ever since she saw him step onto the bus ten years ago.

11:36 pm

Charles smiled as he watched Mariel and Adrian set up decorations. Their parents and Sofia were currently asleep in the chairs across from him, and the two older children were at the gate opposite him, stringing up Christmas lights and taping paper snowflakes to the windows, although there was plenty of real snow outside them.

His smile slipped away as his thoughts once again drifted to his last conversation with Shonda. Maybe Ellen was right, that they were both grieving in their own ways, and it meant that their relationship was bound to be a little rocky while they worked through it. But he also thought of Angie, how much she hated that he and Shonda didn't get along. How much energy she had put into convincing the two of them to talk, making sure their relationship wasn't permanently damaged. He didn't want all that to go to waste.

Charles pulled out his phone, then realized it was almost two in the morning in Atlanta. He texted Shonda. **Call me if you're awake. No rush.**

Less than a minute later, his phone was buzzing. "Hi, Shonda."

"Hey, Dad." Her voice didn't sound like she'd just woken up or anything, which was good. If anything, it sounded wary, as if this might be a trick. "Any updates on the flight?"

"No, still canceled." There was a beat as Charles tried to figure out how to start the conversation he really wanted to have. Shonda filled the silence.

"What's up, then?"

He swallowed, then thought of Angie. She would want this. "I wanted to tell you why I waited to fly out. It doesn't fix anything, but I can at least give you an explanation." Charles gripped the armrest, trying to steady himself.

Shonda was silent for a heartbeat, then said, "Okay. Thanks."

Charles cleared his throat. "I wanted to be here on Christmas Eve, to continue a tradition your mom and I had. Each year we read 'Gift of the Magi' together, and I . . . I couldn't stand the thought of not doing it this year. Of letting it go, even if she was gone. So this morning I went to her grave to read it." He blew out a breath. "It might seem silly, but it felt important to do it."

He rubbed the back of his neck. "And I know you want me to move to Atlanta, but I can't leave your mom behind. Denver, this house—it's where we built our life. I still have plenty of friends here. I'm not alone. And most

223

importantly, it's where she is. I'm not trying to be stubborn or think I always know what's best—although I know I still act like that. I just . . . I don't want to say goodbye to her again." His voice cracked at the end, and while there was more he had planned to say, he couldn't keep talking.

There was quiet, and then Charles heard sniffing. Shonda rarely cried, at least in front of him, but she had been doing it more since Angie had died. It seemed like they were both more fragile without her here to hold them together. "Dad . . . I didn't know. I never meant to take you away from her."

"I know." His voice was gentle, tears now stinging his own eyes.

"And I know you think I'm worrying too much. But . . . it's what Mom wanted."

"What do you mean?" Charles's eyebrows furrowed together.

Shonda swallowed, and her voice was clearer when she spoke again. "Before Mom died . . . she told me to watch out for you. That she was worried about you being all alone after she was gone, and I should take care of you. She said you'd be stubborn, and not want my help, but that I should take care of you anyway." She gave a small laugh. "She kinda called it."

Charles smiled, but stayed silent, thinking about Angie using some of her last time with Shonda to tell her this. Her final attempt to bring the two of them together. "So this is why you've been so pushy."

"I haven't been *pushy*," argued Shonda. "I've just been trying to do what's best for you."

"I can't tell the difference," Charles said with a smile.

Shonda snorted. "Get used to it." There was a beat, and then she said, "Mom loved it here too, you know. And Monica's got her eyes. Jax has her nose. Monica always asks me to do her hair how Gram used to. What I'm trying to say is . . . there are pieces of her here, too."

When Charles swallowed, it was thick with emotion. "I know," he whispered. "You're right. I'll . . . think about moving in with you. I promise. But I'm not ready yet."

Shonda took a long, quavering breath. "Okay. I trust you. You know what's best for you. But I love you, and I'll always worry about you."

"I love you too. And I'll always worry about you. It's sort of my job."

Shonda laughed, but it was shaky. In the pause that followed, Charles watched as people filtered into the gate, no doubt readying for the Christmas party that was starting soon. Eventually, Shonda spoke again. "The tradition you two had . . . I didn't realize there was a story you loved that much."

Charles chuckled. "What does that mean?"

"You know," Shonda said, trying to explain. "You were just so against me studying English, and you've never understood my job as a freelance writer now. I figured you were too . . . stoic for stories, or something."

Now Charles laughed. "I didn't know someone could be too stoic for stories."

Shonda sighed, exasperated, but he thought he heard a smile in her voice. "You know what I mean. Mom was always the one who read and bought me books and then shared my writing with everyone she knew. It didn't seem like your thing."

Now Charles frowned. "Shonda, you know that I read every story you write, right? I may not be much of a reader normally, but whenever you send me a link or share it or whatever, I always read it." He snorted. "I've got so many subscriptions to online publications so I can view your articles, it's a little bit ridiculous."

He had meant the last bit as a joke, but Shonda was quiet for several moments. Her voice was timid when she spoke again. "You . . . you read my stories?"

"Well, sure. I'm your dad. Did you really think I wouldn't read them?" His chest ached. Did she think he care so little about her work?

"But . . . you never said anything. I thought you thought what I did was pointless." Her voice was quivering again.

"I never said anything because we hardly talked. And . . . well, I'm pretty bad at compliments. Your mom never let me forget it." He smiled. "I don't think what you do is pointless. I mean, maybe I thought it was in college, but you're good at it. I just worry about you. If you could get a job at one newspaper or magazine or teach English or something, I would understand that. It's the hopping around from place to place that I don't get." Charles held his breath, unsure if his comment would spark another fight.

"You've never told me that," she said quietly. "I always assumed it was the writing, period. Dad, I do freelance writing in part because it's hard to get a steady job at one publication, but also I sort of enjoy the hustle. I get to write about lots of different things, rather than trying to match my voice or interests to a single publication. Maybe someday I'll do something different, but for now, it's what fits me best."

Charles was quiet. He hadn't realized she enjoyed the frantic nature of her work. If he were being honest, it hadn't even occurred to him that that was a part of work someone *could* enjoy.

"But what if things dry up?" Charles pressed. "If you stop getting jobs or something happens to you and or Jason and one of you can't work?"

"Then we'll figure it out," Shonda said, as if it were that simple. "Listen, at some point I've stayed up all night thinking about every worst-case scenario you could throw at me. But do you really think I could grow up with you as a dad and not know how to budget my money?"

Charles smiled. She had a point. Money had never been overflowing in their household, and he had always taught her the importance of knowing where each dollar came and went. "I figured you always tuned me out."

Shonda laughed. "I tried, but I guess enough of it got through, and now I'm grateful. We have savings, we have a budget, we're doing fine. You raised me to be that way."

A lump formed in Charles's throat. "Well. That's good to know, I guess." He cleared his throat. "I'll try to stop bothering you about money, then. I know you're smart. Your mom and I . . . we've always been proud of you. I hope you know that."

"Thanks, Dad." Shonda took a breath, but it was shaky. "Dad . . . I miss her. So much."

Charles almost couldn't speak, but he forced the words out. "So do I. Christmas was her favorite time of year."

"I tried making those cookies she always made." Shonda laughed weakly. "It didn't feel like Christmas without having them."

"How'd it go?" Charles watched a young couple, two women, wander toward the gate and sit down together, close as two people could be with these airport chairs. He smiled.

Shonda snorted. "Nothing like hers. I followed the recipe exactly, but it was nothing compared to hers."

Charles laughed. "Oh, honey. She never followed the recipe."

A pause. "*What?*"

"Never," Charles laughed. "She got that recipe years ago, then spent decades tweaking it until she perfected it. But she never wrote down any of the changes she made."

"So how did she know how to make it?"

"She just knew. Each year, when it was close to Christmas, she always worried that she'd forgotten how to make them, but once she got in the kitchen, it was like the knowledge was always buried deep in her, and never left."

"But she never wrote it down anywhere? How am I supposed to make them?" Exasperation tinted her voice.

Charles grinned as he crossed one leg over the other. "You'll just have to keep adjusting the recipe until it tastes like what you remember."

"But it won't be Christmas without those cookies," she nearly wailed. He could imagine her slumping down on her couch.

Charles laughed. "For your mom, it was never about the cookies. It was about being in the kitchen baking, unearthing that recipe. It was even more about spending time with you once you were old enough to be in there with her."

He could hear the smile in her voice. "So I should try and bake something anyways. Maybe get the kids to help me."

"I think that sounds like a good idea," Charles said. "I need you here too, though. To help taste test."

Charles smiled. "I'll be there as soon as I can."

11:40 pm

"Okay, only a few more minutes. Anything that we forgot?" Mariel turned to Adrian, hands on her hips. They'd spent the better part of an hour hanging strands of Christmas lights, cutting paper snowflakes and taping them up, organizing the food that various stores had brought, the plates arranged on benches they dragged over and a few display tables some stores had let them borrow. They'd even bought a couple little presents for Sofia and used newspaper to wrap them.

Adrian looked around the gate. "This actually looks pretty dope."

She grinned. "I'm glad you finally noticed." Mariel gazed around as well, evaluating things and mentally ticking off the boxes in her head. Lights, check. Food, check. Gifts, check. Tree— She gasped.

Adrian spun toward her. "What? What is it?"

Mariel's eyes were wide. "A tree! A Christmas tree! We didn't find one—or make one—"

"You *scared* me." Adrian's shoulders relaxed. "So? We've got lots of other stuff. Who needs a tree?"

230

Mariel shook her head as she ran a hand through her thick hair, pulling at the roots. "No, no, we need one. How can it be Christmas without a tree? Where are we supposed to put Sofia's presents?"

"Okay." Adrian held up his hands in a *calm down* gesture. "Then we'll figure something out. We've still got twenty minutes before midnight."

"No!" Mariel said, her voice louder than she meant it to be. Adrian jumped a little. She buried her face in her hands. "That's not enough time! All the stores are closed." She groaned. "What was I thinking? How could I forget a Christmas tree?"

Adrian edged closer, still looking wary after her outburst. "It's seriously not a big deal. Why are you so upset?"

She whirled on him, and he jumped back again. "Because I *care*! Because even though we have to spend Christmas in an airport, I still want it to be fun and for Sofia to remember it as a good memory, not some terrible year where everything went wrong."

Adrian frowned. "I don't think not having a Christmas tree is going to change any of that. It doesn't need to be perfect."

"If it's not going to be perfect, then what's the *point?*" she snapped as she collapsed into a chair.

Adrian stood, hesitating, before lowering himself into the chair next to her. "Mariel . . . are you okay?"

She swallowed, both touched at how gentle he sounded and embarrassed that her little brother was asking her that. "Yeah. I'm fine, sorry. I don't know what that was about." Mariel tried to smile, but it was strained, and she knew her brother noticed.

Adrian was quiet for a moment before speaking. "I know you think because you're the oldest or something you have to keep everything together. But it's not all on you. We're all struggling with this move, and just the fact that you were able to pull this party together in a few hours . . . Sofia and Mom and Dad are gonna love it. You know that, right? That they won't care if a small detail isn't perfect?"

Mariel was silent. A part of her fumed at the fact that her little brother was giving her advice. But another part, a bigger part, thought maybe he was right. Could she really imagine Sofia throwing a fit during the party because there wasn't a Christmas tree? Sofia could be a brat, but she wasn't *that* bad. Mariel's shoulders loosened. "I guess . . . I guess so." She bit her lip. "With everything going on right now—moving, Cole, the flight . . . . I just wanted this one thing to be perfect."

"I noticed." Adrian gave her a teasing grin. "But it's gonna be great. Also . . . " He paused, then forged on. "You realize your ex was trash, right?"

Mariel started, then turned toward him. "What? I thought you liked Cole?"

Adrian snorted. "Mom made me promise not to be a jerk to him. But he . . . " Adrian shook his head. "He was

232

so rude and stuck up. I don't know how you handled it." He gripped his knees, tight enough that his knuckles turned pale. "I got so mad. He would talk to you like you were, I don't know, a little kid or something, and you would let him. I never understood it. You deserved—you still deserve—someone way better than that. I might just be your little brother, but even I know that." He paused, and Mariel could tell he was thinking about something else for a minute.

It gave her the chance to think about what he'd said. Was he right? Was Cole really that bad? She reflected on their relationship. The reason she'd ever had a crush on him was because they were in all the same advanced placement classes, and he always seemed to have something smart to say. But as she thought about it more, she remembered all the times he interrupted people to give his answer. All the time they spent hanging out where it was only him talking, and her listening and nodding. How she learned to not bother to try and add her own opinion, because he either drowned it out or shot it down. How she hesitated to show him things that were her favorites—movies, books, TV shows—because he might criticize and ridicule it. She swallowed. How had she missed that?

When she looked back up at Adrian, he had come out of his own thoughts. She smiled at him. "I think . . . I think you're right."

Adrian held up his arms in a victory pose. "Whoa! Did everyone hear that?" he called to nobody. He twisted to

233

face her. "I need you to say that again, so I can record it, please."

She rolled her eyes, shoving his shoulder. "Don't ruin it, jerk." Adrian grinned at her. She raised an eyebrow as she settled back in the chair. "All right, all right. What about you and June? What happened there?"

It was like Adrian folded in on himself. "She's back with her ex."

Mariel frowned, leaning forward again. "Really? That's weird. She definitely seemed into you whenever I saw you two."

Adrian shook his head, studying the carpet under their feet. "There was never anything there. I should have never hung out with her. There was no way it was going to end well."

"What does that mean?" Mariel asked, brows furrowed.

Adrian shrugged, kicking a shoe on the ground. "I've never clicked with anyone. I thought maybe I did with June, but obviously I was wrong. Why would she be any different than anybody else I've met?"

"Um, because she's her own person?" Mariel said with a snort. Adrian turned to face her. "I'm telling you, she was flirting with you. I don't know about this whole thing with her ex, but just because other people have let you down doesn't mean she will."

Adrian was going to respond, but then Mariel noticed someone approaching from behind him. Before she had fully registered the red hair flashing, Mariel was getting to her feet. Adrian stood too, a frown on his face.

"Ah—I'm gonna go wake up Mom and Dad," she said.

As she walked by Adrian, she squeezed his shoulder and whispered to him, "Don't screw this up."

Confusion colored Adrian's features as he turned to follow her, and came face to face with June.

11:47 pm

When Keely reached their gate, she saw the two teens decorating a nearby gate with Christmas decorations. She remembered the announcement a couple hours ago inviting everyone to the party, and smiled. It was a cute idea.

Right now, though, her mind was focused on something else. Namely, the text she'd gotten from Wes a little bit earlier: **Meet me at the gate?**

She considered not going. She was still upset at him. But in the couple hours since their fight, she had also cooled off some. It had started when she'd opened Facebook and saw her "memories" post from a year ago: a photo of Wes dressed up as Santa for their friends' kids at a Christmas party. He looked so goofy, and all the kids were beaming. Keely was in the background, clutching her stomach as she laughed.

She remembered how much fun that night had been, seeing him impersonate Santa and make every kid laugh. Wes had always been good with kids; maybe she should have guessed that no matter what he said, he would eventually want some of his own. But that aside, the photo

236

reminded her of how much fun they always had together. Of why she had married the goofball in the first place. She hadn't changed her mind about kids, but she did feel bad for yelling at him. She loved him still, and they were adults. They should be able to talk through things like this. So when he texted her, she made her way to the gate of their canceled flight.

Keely spotted Wes sitting in a row of chairs that faced the dark windows. She took a steadying breath before walking toward him.

Wes looked up at her approach. His face shifted, from the detached boredom of looking at his phone to nervousness to . . . something else. Keely couldn't tell what. She hoped it was something good.

"Hey," she said, tucking a piece of hair behind her ear. "Can I sit down?"

"Yeah, of course." He grabbed his bag off the seat next to him, and Keely settled into it.

"So," she said, twisting in the chair to look at him.

"So," he repeated. Keely bit her lip. She didn't think either of them had been this nervous to talk to each other since they first started dating.

Wes cleared his throat, and then spoke. "Okay. Here it is. I'm sorry. You've always been upfront about what you wanted, which is one of the things I love about you. So I should have known if you wanted kids, you would have told me. It wasn't fair of me to be mad at you for being who you've always been. And I'm sorry that it ruined what should have been a happy moment when you found out about the job." Wes fidgeted with the edge of his sleeve. "But I also still want kids. And I don't know what that means for us."

Keely's breath caught. "I'm sorry, too," she said. "I was so mad at you, when we should have talked about it, instead of yelling. I just felt so betrayed." She reached out to grab his hand. "I love you. I want to do life with you, whether it's in Arizona or England. But . . . I don't want kids. That hasn't changed, and I don't think it ever will."

Wes nodded, but the motion was stiff. Dimly, she registered people laughing in the background, gathering for the party, but the sounds were muted, as if she and Wes were underwater.

Her eyes searched his. "Am I enough? Is what we have, right now, enough?"

"Of course." Wes squeezed her hand. "I shouldn't have said that. You will always be enough." He smiled, but it reminded her of a wilted flower.

Keely swallowed. "But you still want kids." Wes nodded. "So . . . where do we go from here?"

Wes shook his head. "I don't know." The words were nearly a whisper, choked with emotion.

She laid her head on his shoulder. He pressed his lips into her hair. And they sat like that, staring at the plunging darkness outside the windows, not speaking as the snow continued to fall.

11:52 pm

As Mariel hurried past him, Adrian turned, and saw June standing there. His heart started beating so fast he thought it might burst out of his chest, but at the same time his stomach dropped. Why was she back? *Thank goodness she's back.*

Adrian swallowed and faced her, trying to keep the emotion out of his voice as he asked, "What do you want?"

June's arms were crossed in front of her chest, and as Adrian looked at her, she seemed determined, almost angry, not glowing like she had been after talking with Kaden. He didn't know what to make of that.

As an answer, June simple said, "*Golden Hollow* issue number one." Her voice was steady, revealing no emotion.

Adrian frowned, racking his brain. "*The Foggy Falconer?*"

She nodded. "Kell assists Detective Martin as a specialist for one case, and then she wants to keep working with him because they make a good team." June raised an eyebrow, and Adrian's mouth opened a little as he remembered the plot. "But he won't let her, because his last partner betrayed him . . . "

"And he doesn't want to get hurt again," Adrian finished. His palms started sweating.

June let her arms drop as she marched closer to him. She was a few inches shorter than him, but somehow she still managed to look him in the eye. "Be straight with me. Are you Detective Martin-ing me?"

Adrian opened his mouth, then shut it again. Finally he squeaked out, "Maybe?" He cleared his throat. "But . . . it's not just that. I want you to be happy. Even if that meant it wasn't with me. I didn't understand, but I wanted you to be happy. But." Adrian took a deep breath, thinking of how he'd told Mariel she deserved better. Of how she reminded him to give June the chance to choose. She couldn't do that if she didn't know how he felt.

"I . . . I think you could be happy with me." As he spoke the words, his heart pounded like it had when he first jumped off the high dive at the swimming pool years ago. "I don't know what sort of history you and Kaden have, and I know you've only known me for a few hours, but you deserve better than some jerk who cheats on you and doesn't realize how amazing you are." He could feel his cheeks heating up, but he plunged ahead. "You deserve someone who knows that your left eye crinkles up more than your right one when you smile. Who gets your inside jokes about Golden Hollow. Who knows that you've been through a lot, but you've still got this . . . lightness in you, that makes other people happy just by being around you. You deserve someone who sees you and knows you and would never let you go," Adrian finished. June looked as stunned as he felt.

In the heartbeat that followed his unexpected speech, Adrian swore the airport, and maybe the world, froze, like everything was holding its breath with him as he waited for June to reply.

And then she said, "I know."

Adrian blinked. That . . . wasn't what he had expected.

She smiled at him, soft and secret, her left eye crinkling a little more than her right. "You're right. I deserve someone better than Kaden. That's why, when I called him earlier, I dumped him. And I was going to tell you that it was over and that I liked you, but then you walked away. So I'm a little confused what this speech is all about."

"You—I—" Adrian fumbled for words. "But I heard you talking. You said . . . you said you missed him and loved him and couldn't wait to see him again."

Now June frowned. "Were you eavesdropping?"

"No—I mean, yes, but not on purpose. It took you awhile, so I got worried and went to check on you. Then I overheard the end of your conversation," Adrian explained in a hurry, hoping to wipe the confused and hurt look off of June's face. "When you came back looking so happy, I thought Kaden must have explained and apologized, and you forgave him. I didn't want to stand in the way of you feeling that way."

Confusion clouded June's face for a moment longer, and then it cleared. She started laughing. Adrian froze, unsure what this meant. Finally, June managed to say, "You dork! My *mom* called me right after I hung up with Kaden. *That's* the conversation you overhead." Her laughter quieted, and she met his gaze. "The reason I was so happy when I saw you was because . . . well, because I saw *you.*"

Oh. *Oh.*

Adrian silently cursed himself for being so thoughtless. "I'm sorry," he said. "I should have listened to you, instead of assuming. But . . . " There was still the *other* reason they shouldn't date. "Even still, we'll eventually leave this airport and be on opposite sides of the world. It's not like we're on opposite coasts of the U.S. for a semester or something. I'm moving to a whole new country, and I don't know if or when I'll be able to come back. And Spain is, like, six hours ahead of Atlanta." He shook his head. "I don't see how it can work."

June chewed her lip. "I didn't say it would be easy. But I'm not ready to give up on you. Hanging out with you today was the happiest I've been in a long time. We get each other. I don't want to lose that." Her shoulders hunched a little, as if she were protecting herself from an anticipated attack. "If you don't feel the same, then that's . . . fine. But if you *do* feel that way and you're just scared that you'll hurt me or I'll hurt you, then I'm asking you. Please don't give up on us because you're afraid. I'm willing to fight to make this work. Are you?"

Adrian stood, staring at her. He traced how her hair flowed over her shoulders, how her eyes searched his, how her lips were the perfect shade of pink. He remembered laughing with her today until he could barely breathe. He remembered how natural and comfortable it was to sit in silence as they read together. He remembered the happiness that sparkled in her as she came around the corner, that he now realized was aimed at *him*. Was he willing to fight for that?

"Okay, everybody!" Mariel's voice carried across the surrounding gates as she stood on a chair in the line of seats between gates. "It's one minute away from midnight, which means it's one minute away from Christmas!" A cheer went up from the crowd that had gathered, but Adrian's eyes were locked on June. "We set up this party for our little sister, Sofia, but I think everyone is going to enjoy it. Let's count down to Christmas!"

"Ten! Nine! Eight!" The crowd chanted with Mariel.

Adrian took a step towards June. Then another. His heart was pounding and his hands were clammy, but something deeper than all that inside him felt sure. He stood in front of June. With a small smile, she nodded upward. "Look."

Adrian tilted his head back to look at the ceiling above them. A branch of mistletoe hung from the ceiling tiles—where had Mariel even gotten that? It didn't matter.

Adrian looked back down at June, and before he could talk himself out of it, he leaned forward and kissed her.

"One! Merry Christmas!"

Cheers went up all around them, but June and Adrian were lost in their own world.

Midnight

Mariel meandered through the crowd, unable to contain the smile on her face. Everyone was chatting and looking happier than she'd seen all night. It was a weird Christmas, to be sure, but there was a buzz in the air that made it feel special.

"Mariel! Mariel!" Sofia came sprinting toward her. Mariel laughed and braced herself in time for Sofia to tackle her with a giant hug. "This. Is. Awesome!" she shouted in Mariel's ear. Mariel winced a little, but her smile didn't falter.

"I'm glad you like it." Mariel squeezed Sofia. Her parents made their way toward them.

"This is beautiful, Mariel," Mom said as Mariel set Sofia down. "I'm impressed you were able to get it all together."

"It was a group effort." Mariel smiled at them, and then caught sight of Charles chatting with some people over their shoulder. She swallowed, but thought about her conversation with Adrian. Maybe she didn't have to do everything on her own.

"Mom, Dad . . . after this is over, can we talk about something?" she asked. Immediately, worry creased their faces. "No, nothing bad, like that. I'm just . . . feeling nervous about moving, and I don't feel like we've ever really talked about it."

Dad nodded and put his hand on Mariel's shoulder. "Of course. Let's talk later."

Mariel smiled gratefully, then turned to Sofia. "Did you see your gifts yet?"

Mariel didn't think it was possible for Sofia's eyes to get any wider, but they did. "I can open them now? I don't have to wait till the morning?" she asked, bouncing on her toes.

"Nope." Mariel grinned. "C'mon, follow me." Mariel took her sister's hand and led her through the people who had gathered. She spotted Kat drinking sodas and looking very cozy with a tall guy, who she assumed was the friend she had talked about. Kat caught her eye, and lifted her can in a sort of salute to Mariel, who grinned back. A glance back told her Charles was talking to her parents, all three of them laughing together, which eased tension in her chest a little bit.

"Where are we going?" asked Sofia, almost dancing with excitement, her eyes wide.

"They're right over here." Mariel led her to a stack of gifts wrapped in newspaper.

She chewed on her lip, still wishing they'd made a tree of some sort, but Sofia squealed with delight. "Can I open them?"

"Go for it," Mariel said. "Adrian helped pick them out, but I don't know where he is . . . " She trailed off. As Sofia dived for the first present, Mariel saw Adrian with his arm around June's shoulder, sitting a little ways off. She smiled. Good. She liked June.

"A buffalo!" yelled Sofia, holding up the fuzzy stuffed buffalo that was her first gift. "I love it! I'll name him . . . George." Mariel couldn't help but laugh as Sofia ripped into the next gift. "My favorite color!" Sofia held up the purple T-shirt with a drawing of mountains on it.

"I know, kid, that's why we chose it." Mariel laughed, gathering the discarded newspaper and crumpling it into one large ball. "Open the last one."

Two women were standing nearby at the table of food provided by Trevor from The Slice, snacking on garlic knots. As Mariel watched, one leaned forward and kissed the other's nose, and she giggled and covered her mouth. Even though they were in the middle of an airport, the moment seemed intimate, and Mariel turned away.

"Books!" Sofia said, looking at a box with a stack of picture books Mariel had gotten from the Tattered Cover location. She looked up at Mariel, her forehead creased. "But I'm not good at reading."

"Who told you that?" Mariel bent down to get on her level. "You're a great reader, and you'll only get better with time. I bet by the time we've reached Spain, you'll have read all these books and be ready for new ones."

She tossed the ball of newspaper at Sofia, who squealed with delight, then wrapped her arms around Mariel's neck in a hug. "Thank you, thank you!"

Mariel hugged her sister back, smiling widely. She felt like she was overflowing with emotions, happiness and joy and still the undercurrent of worry about what the future held, but right now, in this moment, she couldn't imagine anything better.

"Excuse me."

Mariel stood up and turned at the sound of the voice behind her. For a second, she couldn't think of why the woman looked so familiar. Then her eyes widened. It was the gate attendant who they'd tricked into leaving the mic so Mariel could make the invitation announcement. Victoria, according to her name tag.

"Um . . . hi?" Mariel squeaked out. Was she really about to get put in airport-jail on Christmas Eve? Was that even a thing? They had to have some place where they put people who broke the rules—was that her? Mariel's palms began to sweat.

Victoria raised an eyebrow. "You're the one who organized this?"

Mariel nodded. Like she had told her parents, it was a group effort, but she decided not to throw Adrian and June under the bus. Yet.

Sofia tugged on her hand. "What's happening?"

"Shh, why don't you play with your new toys?" Mariel said quietly, hardly daring to glance down at her sister. She met Victoria's gaze as Sofia took a few steps back, but didn't leave. "It was my idea."

Victoria nodded. Mariel swallowed, waiting to see security guards emerge from the crowd to take her away. But then Victoria said, "Well, do you want me to show you how to use the system to play music?"

Mariel blinked. Once. Twice. "What?" Was this a joke?

Victoria smiled, as if enjoying Mariel's confusion. "For the party. You did good, but I think all the best parties need some music and dancing, don't you?"

Mariel could hardly believe what she heard. "You're not mad? Am I in trouble?"

Victoria's grin widened. "No, of course not. It's Christmas Eve—well, Christmas Day now. I was mad for a few minutes, but then everyone in the airport was talking about how fun the idea of a Christmas party was, and. . . . " She shrugged. "How could I be mad at that?"

Mariel's legs felt like jelly. "Oh—well, that's great!" Victoria's earlier offer suddenly clicked in her head. "So we can play music?"

Victoria nodded. "Follow me."

A few minutes later, Victoria had showed Mariel how to hook up her phone to the announcement system. She scrolled through her music library, trying to decide on the perfect song, one that could capture all the emotions swirling in her right now: still hurting from a hard couple of months, but triumphant and thankful for where she was right now, and maybe even a tiny bit excited for what was to come.

When the first few notes blared through the speakers, most people in attendance stopped and looked around. Mariel waved at them, and they grinned back at her.

The two women who had been so cozy together earlier were talking animatedly now, near enough to the gate that she caught snippets.

"Landry, come dance with me!" the dark-haired woman said, grabbing the other woman's hand.

"Resa . . . " Landry said, her uncertainty plain in her voice.

But Resa tugged at Landry until she set down her drink and followed her to an empty space among the chairs. Resa started dancing, singing the lyrics at Landry, who laughed and eventually sang them with her girlfriend, the two jumping up and down together. Kat and her boyfriend joined in, and he twirled Kat in circles until she was gasping with giggles. Other guests trickled in, until they had a full-fledged dance party. Even the couple who had been sitting quietly facing the windows got up to dance, though they kept more to themselves.

Mariel turned to grin at Victoria, who was also watching the party approvingly. They high-fived.

Mariel's phone buzzed. When she checked it, she saw it was the Girls Who Code group chat.

How are you doing, M? Candice had asked.

Mariel looked up from the screen to survey the scene in front of her. June was leading Adrian toward the dance party, both of them radiating with happiness. She even saw her parents on the edge of the large group, dancing with Sofia, who was shrieking with laughter.

Smiling, Mariel typed out a response to the group: **I've never been better.**

Then she locked her phone and went to join the dance party. Cheers went up as she neared, making her feel like a celebrity. She jumped and sang and danced with her family and with strangers and with people she'd met tonight who already felt like family. At one point, she grabbed Sofia's hands, and they spun in circles together, both barely able to breathe from laughing so hard, twirling and spinning until they felt like they were part of the snowflakes swirling outside.

Acknowledgements

    It's something of a misnomer to say this book was independently published. While I may have done it independently from a publishing company, I could not have completed it without the help and encouragement of many, many people.

    First and foremost, I couldn't do anything without the grace of Jesus Christ. Thank You for giving me my love of storytelling and surrounding me with people who have encouraged me to pursue that love.

    Thank you to my writing community, IRL and online. The Boulder Writer's Alliance, Boulder Writing Dates, the Create If Writing group, the Young Writer's Community — you've made me a better writer and gave me the space to actually sit down and write. To the All Souls Writers Guild, thank you for helping these stories be so much better than they were when they started. And for making it possible for me to say I'm part of a guild.

    To my team of beta readers, thank you for seeing these characters and this story in their very rough forms and giving me so much advice and encouragement to make them come alive.

A huge thanks to my sensitivity readers Melissa and Cath — your kind and honest comments have made me a better writer and person, and made many of these characters authentic and true in a way I couldn't do on my own. To Kyle DeMarco for taking my vague idea of a Christmassy illustrated cover and turning it into something better than I could have dreamed of. You deserve all the donuts and Coke Zeroes.

Of course, I owe so much to people who may not be writers but are still in some way responsible for this book coming into existence. To all my friends, old and new, spread out across the world — all the shared laughter and tears and inside jokes and late night conversations have made me who I am and helped me to grow as a person and as a creator. To my family who has never doubted my dream to be an author. Madison and Chandler, the Addis siblings in this book may not seem like us on the surface, but they would defend each other to the death, and that bond comes from y'all. Dad, thank you for instilling a love of stories in me — you'll always be Storyman. Mom, thank you for never letting me give up on my dream of being an author, even when it seemed so far way, and for always bingeing Hallmark Christmas movies with me.

Sam, all the ways you made this book possible could fill another entire book. Thank you for working harder than Santa's elves to keep the house in order while I locked myself away to write. Thanks for talking me through plot holes and characters who wouldn't cooperate and my breakdowns when I was convinced I was a fraud who couldn't actually write. You are my happily ever after.

And of course, dear reader, thank you. As a self-published author, I am so, so aware of how much of my success depends on people like you taking a chance on this book. I can't thank you enough for choosing to take a chance on me.

Finally, to 2020. When I decided back in January I wanted to write a book, I had no idea what was coming. You've been a rough year in a lot of different ways. But you'll always be the year I published my first book. So at least there's that.

About the Author

Chelsea Pennington lives in Colorado with her husband and their dog, Pippin. Her first story was Pokémon fanfiction in kindergarten, and she's been writing ever since. When she's not writing or reading, you can probably find her listening to podcasts or hiking. This is her first novel. You can connect with Chelsea online at www.chelseapenningtonauthor.com, where you can also find a short story epilogue to your favorite characters from *The Mistletoe Connection*.